Da Vinc

W9-DGP-835

JOHNS HOPKINS:
POETRY AND FICTION

JOHN T. IRWIN
general editor

Da Vinci's Bicycle

Ten Stories by Guy Davenport

The Johns Hopkins University Press
BALTIMORE AND LONDON

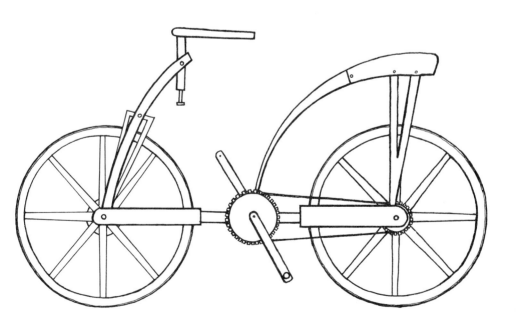

This book has been brought to publication
with the generous assistance of the G. Harry Pouder Fund.

Manufactured in the United States of America

The Johns Hopkins University Press, Baltimore, Maryland 21218
The Johns Hopkins Press, Ltd., London

Library of Congress Catalog Number 78–20513
ISBN 0–8018–2208–4 (hardcover)
ISBN 0–8018–2220–3 (paperback)

Library of Congress Cataloging in Publication data
will be found on the last printed page of this book.

To the memory of
LOUIS ZUKOFSKY
1904 · 1978

Contents

Acknowledgments

The drawing of Leonardo da Vinci's bicycle on the title page is derived, with structural reinterpretation in the fork and seat strut, from Antonio Calegari's model in Augusto Marinoni's "The Bicycle," *The Unknown Leonardo*, edited by Ladislao Reti (McGraw-Hill, 1974), and appears here with the kind permission of the publisher. Professor Calegari's model is based on the recently discovered drawing by Salai Jacopo dei Caprotti (aet. 11, *circa* 1493) of a bicycle drawn or perhaps built by Leonardo.

The final paragraphs of "Au Tombeau de Charles Fourier," beginning with "Everybody was on the streets," are from Gertrude Stein's *The Autobiography of Alice B. Toklas*. For the parts about the cosmology of the Dogon I am indebted to Marcel Griaule's *Dieu d'Eau: entretiens avec Ogotemmêli* (1948) and his and Germaine Dieterlen's *Le Renard pâle* (1965). The drawing of the Wright Flyer No. 1 (Signal Corps Aircraft No. 1) is derived from a drawing by Peter F. Copeland, chief of the Illustration Department, NASM, Smithsonian Institution. The athlete in the *collages* is from photographs by Erik A. Ruby in his *The Human Figure* (Van Nostrand Reinhold, 1974). The drawing of James Joyce is from a photograph by Gisèle Freund. The drawing of the young Lartigue is from a photograph by his father.

The drawings accompanying "The Invention of Photography in Toledo" are derived from Edward S. Curtis (the Mohave girl), Nadar (Rossini), and a photograph of the young Van Gogh (*circa* 1866) in the possession of Pastor J. P. Scholte-van Houten, Lochem. For the title of this story I am indebted to the poet Robert Kelly, who read a book so named in a dream.

[xi]

All but one of these stories have appeared before in journals, and grateful acknowledgment is herewith made to their editors for permission to reprint. "A Field of Snow on a Slope of the Rosenberg," © 1977 by the University of Georgia, originally appeared in the Spring 1977 issue of *The Georgia Review*; "Au Tombeau de Charles Fourier," © 1975 by the University of Georgia, originally appeared in the Winter 1975 issue of *The Georgia Review*. Both stories are reprinted by permission of *The Georgia Review*. Permission to reprint was also granted by *Parenthèse* for "The Invention of Photography in Toledo" and "The Wooden Dove of Archytas," by *The Hawaii Review* for "The Richard Nixon Freischütz Rag" (also published in *Prize Stories 1976: The O. Henry Awards*, edited by William Abrahams [Doubleday & Co., 1976]), by *Mulch* for "The Haile Selassie Funeral Train," by *The Hudson Review* for "C. Musonius Rufus" and "The Antiquities of Elis," and by *The Kenyon Review* for "John Charles Tapner."

Da Vinci's Bicycle

The Richard Nixon
Freischütz Rag

ON THE Great Ten Thousand Li Wall, begun in the wars of the
Spring and Autumn to keep the Mongols who had been camping
nearer and nearer the Yan border from riding in hordes on their
przhevalskis into the cobbled streets and ginger gardens of the
Middle Flower Kingdom, Richard Nixon said:

— I think you would have to conclude that this is a great wall.

Invited by Marshal Yeh Chien-ying to inspect a guard tower
on the ramparts, he said:

— We will not climb to the top today.

In the limousine returning to the Forbidden City, he said:

— It is worth coming sixteen thousand miles to see the Wall.

Of the tombs of the Ming emperors, he said:

— It is worth coming to see these, too.

— Chairman Mao says, Marshal Yeh ventured, that the past is
past.

The translator had trouble with the sentiment, which lost its
pungency in English.

— All over? Richard Nixon asked.

— We have poem, Marshal Yeh said, which I recite.

> West wind keen,
> Up steep sky
> Wild geese cry
> For dawn moon.
>
> For cold dawn
> White with frost,

[1]

When horse neigh,
Bugle call.

Boast not now
This hard pass
Was like iron
Underfoot.

At the top
We see hills
And beyond
The red sun.

Richard Nixon leaned with attention, grinning, to hear the translation from the interpreter, Comrade Tang Wen-Sheng, whose English had been learned in Brooklyn, where she spent her childhood.

— That's got to be a good poem, Richard Nixon said.

— Poem by Chairman Mao, Comrade Tang offered.

— He wrote that? Richard Nixon asked. Made it up?

— At hard pass over Mountain Lu, Marshal Yeh said. Long March. February 1935.

— My! but that's interesting, Richard Nixon said. Really, really interesting.

The limousine slid past high slanting gray walls of The Forbidden City on which posters as large as tennis courts bore writing Richard Nixon could not read. They proclaimed, poster after poster by which the long limousine moved, *Make trouble, fail. Again make trouble, again fail. Imperialist reactionary make trouble and fail until own destruction. Thought of Chairman Mao.*

The limousine stopped at The Dragon Palace. Richard Nixon got out. Guards of the Heroic People's Volunteer Army stood at attention. On a wall inside the courtyard four tall posters caught the eye of Richard Nixon.

— That's Marx, he said, pointing.

— Marx, repeated Marshal Yeh.

— And that's Engels.

— Engels.

— And that's Lenin and that's Stalin.

— Precisely, Marshal Yeh replied.

Richard Nixon went back to the second poster, pointing to it with his gloved hand.

— That's Engels?

— Engels, Marshal Yeh said with a worried, excessively polite look in his eyes.

— We don't see many pictures of Engels in America, Richard Nixon explained.

THAT MAN old Toscanelli put up to sailing to the Japans and Cathay westward out from Portugal, the Genovese Colombo, they have been saying around the Uffizi, has come back across the Atlantic. *Una pròva elegantissima!* Benedetto Arithmetic would say. The Aristotelians will be scandalized, *di quale se fanno beffa.* The Platonists will fluff their skirts and freeze the air with their lifted noses. *È una stella il mundo!* But like the moon, forsooth, round as a melon, plump and green. O, he could see those *caravelle* butting salt and savage waves, the awful desert of water and desolation of the eye, until the unimaginable shorebirds of Cipongo wheeled around their sails and the red tiles and bamboo *pèrgole* of Mongol cities came into focus on capes and promontories. Inland, there were roads out to Samarkand, India, Persia, Hungary, Helvetia, and thus back to Tuscany.

He had completed the world journey of the Magi, it occurred to Leonardo as he moved the bucket of grasses which Salai had brought him from Fiesole. They had come from the East, astrologers, and Colombo's sails in these days of signs wherein every moving thing must declare itself for God or Islam would have worn the cross which the philosophers of the Medes did not wait to learn would be forever until the end of time the hieroglyph of the baby before whom they laid their gifts in the dark stable. The world was knit by prophecy, by light.

Meadow grass from Fiesole, icosahedra, cogs, gears, plaster, maps, lutes, brushes, an adze, magic squares, pigments, a Roman head Brunelleschi and Donatello brought him from their excavations, the skeleton of a bird: how beautifully the Tuscan light gave him his things again every morning, even if the kite had been in his sleep.

Moments, hour, days. Had man done anything at all?

The old woman had brought the wine and the bread, the onions. He and Toscanelli, Pythagoreans, ate no meat.

The machine stood against the worktable, the *due rote*, unaccountably outrageous in design. Saccapane the smith was making the chain that would span the two *rote dentate*. You turned the pedals with your feet, which turned the big cog wheel, which pulled the chain forward, cog by cog, causing the smaller wheel to turn the hind *rota*, thereby propelling the whole machine forward. As long as the machine was in motion, the rider would balance beautifully. The forward motion stole away any tendency to fall right or left, as the flow of a river discouraged a boat from wandering.

If only he knew the languages! He could name his machines as Archimède would have named them, in the ancient words. He called his flying machine the bird, *l'uccello*. Benedetto said that the Greeks would have called it an *ornitottero*, the wings of a bird.

Light with extravagance and precision, mirror of itself *atomo per atomo* from its dash against the abruptness of matter to the jelly of the eye, swarmed from high windows onto the two-wheeled balancing machine. The rider would grasp horns set on the fork in which the front wheel was fixed and thus guide himself with nervous and accurate meticulousness. Suddenly he saw the Sforze going into battle on it, a phalanx of these *due rote* bearing lancers at full tilt. *Avanti O Coraggiosi, O!* the trumpet called, *tambureggiandi le bacchette delli tamburi di battaglia.*

The scamp Salai was up and about.

— *Maestro!* he piped. You've made it!

Leonardo picked up the brown boy Salai, shouldered him like a sack of flour, and danced the long gliding steps of a sarabande.

— *Sì, Cupidello mio, tutto senonchè manca la catena.*

— And then I can make it go, ride it like a pony?

— Like the wind, like Ezekiel's angel, like the horses of Ancona.

Salai squirmed free and knelt before the strange machine, touching the pedals, the wicker spokes, the saddle, the toothed wheels around which the chain would fit, *i vinci*.

— *Como leone!*

He turned to the basket of flowering grasses, reaching for his silver pencil. Bracts and umbrels fine as a spider's legs! And in the thin green veins ran hairs of water, and down the hairs of water ran light, down into the dark, into the root. Light from the farthest stars flowed through these long leaves. He had seen the prints of leaves from the time of the flood in mountain rocks, and had seen there shells from the sea.

— Maestro, Salai said, when will the chain be ready?

— Chain? Leonardo asked. What chain?

He drew with his left hand a silver eddy of grass. It was grace that he drew, perfection, frail leaves through which moved the whole power of God, and when a May fly lights on a green arc of grass the splendor of that conjunction is no less than San Gabriele touching down upon the great Dome at Byzantium, closing the crushed silver and spun glass of his four wings around the golden shaft of his height.

— The chain, Salai said, the chain!

Did man know anything at all?

BEFORE FLYING to China Richard Nixon ordered a thousand targets in Laos and Cambodia bombed by squadrons of B-52s. He sent a hundred and twenty-five squadrons of bombers to silence the long-range field guns of North Viet Nam along the border of the DMZ. Richard Nixon was pleased with the bombing, knowing that Chairman Mao would be impressed by such power. Dr. Kissinger had recommended the one thousand, one hundred and twenty-five squadrons of bombers to Richard Nixon as something that would impress Chairman Mao. The bombs were falling thick as hail in a summer storm when Richard Nixon set foot on China, grinning. A band played The March of the Volunteers. Premier Chou En-lai did not walk forward. Richard Nixon had to walk to where Premier Chou stood grinning. They shook hands.

— We came by way of Guam, Richard Nixon said. It is better that way.

— You have good trip? Premier Chou asked.

— You should know, Richard Nixon said. You are such a traveler.

Richard Nixon rode in a limosuine to Taio Yu Tai, outside The Forbidden City. As soon as he got to his room, the telephone rang.

— Who would be calling me in China? he asked.

Dr. Kissinger answered the telephone.

— Yes? he said.

— Excellency Kissinger? a voice asked. You are there?

— We are here, Dr. Kissinger said.

— His Excellency the President Nixon is there?

— Right here, said Dr. Kissinger, taking off his shoes.

— Would His Excellency Nixon come to telephone?

— Sure, said Dr. Kissinger. For you, Dick.

Richard Nixon took the telephone, put it to his ear, and looked at the ceiling, where scarlet dragons swam through clouds of pearl.

— Nixon here, he said.

— Excellency President Nixon there?

— Right here, Richard Nixon said. To who have I the honor of addressing?

— Now you speak with Comrade Secretary Wang.

A new voice came on the line. It said:

— Chairman Mao invite you, now, come to visit him.

— Right now? Richard Nixon asked. We've just got off the plane. We came by way of Guam.

— Now, said the telephone. You come visit. Yes?

— OK, Richard Nixon said. Will do. You coming to pick us up? The line had gone dead.

— Son of a bitch, Richard Nixon said.

Dr. Kissinger rocked on his heels and grinned from ear to ear.

ROSES, BUTTONS, thimbles, lace. The grass grows up to the stones, the road. There are flowers in the grass and flowers on her dress. And buttons down her dress, and lace on the collar and cuffs and hem. And buttons on her shoes. In the Luxembourg she wears a shawl from Segovia and Pablo says she looks like a Spanish woman of the old school, when women were severe and well bred and kind, and I say that she looks like an officer in the Union Army. We sing *The Trail of the Lonesome Pine* which she plays on the piano, throwing in snatches of *Marching through Georgia* and *Alexander's Ragtime Band*. She has Pumpelly's nose, the hands of a Spanish saint.

In France she wears a yellow hat, in Italy a Panama. Alice, I say, Assisi, the grass of Assisi, and the leaves Sassetta. We walk comfortably over the stones, hearing the bells ring for the nuns and the girls in their school. It is so quiet, she says, being herself quiet to say that it is quiet. Spain is a still life, I say, only Italy is landscape. The birds there, she says. St. Francis, I say. The birds suffer their suffering each in a lifetime, forgetting it as they endure. We remember suffering from years and years ago. Do not talk of old things, she says. There is no time anymore, only now. Not, say I, if you can hear as I can the bugles and see the scarlet flags.

And I could, I can, I always can. The officers sit in their saddles and the guidons with their Victorian numbers and faded reds move to the head of the column. It is an old way with men, it happened at Austerlitz and Sevastopol. The generals are high on their horses, listening to the band, to the shouts of the sergeants. It is glory. When Leo moved out, we trotted around the room like horses, and Basket went around with us. I was the general and Alice was the officer and Basket was the horse, and altogether we were Napoleon. We were pickaninnies cakewalking before the elders on a Saturday in Alabama, we were Barnum and Bailey and the Great Rat of Sumatra going a progress to Chantilly to see the lace and the cream.

It is quiet, she says, and I say Alice, look at the flowers. Yes, she says. Yes, I say. Is it not grand to say *yes* back and forth when we mean something else and she went behind the bush and loosened her stays and camisole and shamelessly stepped out of the frilly heap they made around her buttoned shoes and I said *yes*, here where St. Francis walked, Alice, you do realize, don't you, that the reason we came to Assisi is that you are from San Francisco and this is the hometown of St. Francis and she says I am wrapping my underthings in my shawl, do you think anyone will notice?

Red tile, moss, pigeons. We drink wine under the trees, though it is too hot to drink wine. Well, I say, we are here. Yes, she says, we are here, and her eyes jiggle and her smile is that of a handsome officer who has been called to headquarters and seen General Grant and is pleased to please, well bred that he is.

This is not Fouquet's, I say. Certainly not Fouquet's, she says. I touch her foot with my foot, she touches my foot with her foot. The crickets sing around us, fine as Stravinsky. If Spain is a still life, what is Italy? They came here, I said, the grand old poets, because the women have such eyes. Surely not to see the cats, Alice says. No, I say, not for the cats. Henry James came here for the tone. William might come here and never see the tone. William if he came would take in the proportions, and would not look at the cats. A princess and a cart go by, Henry sees the princess and William sees the wheel of the cart how it is in such fine proportion to the tongue and the body.

When you talk, she says, I shiver all over, things flutter around inside. When you smile, I say, I bite into peaches and Casals plays Corelli and my soul is a finch in cherries. Let us talk and smile forever. This is forever, Alice says. It is so quiet. Look at the dust, I say. Would you walk in it barefoot? Another glass of wine, she says, and I will fly over the bell tower. Did you have a rosewood piano in San Francisco? I ask. With a bust of Liszt on it, she says, and a vase of marigolds.

Look at these colors and you can see why Sassetta was Sassetta. Will we go to England again, she says, to sit in the cathedrals? Look at these hills and you will know why St. Francis was St. Francis.

The roses, she says, are very old. They are the roses of Ovid, I say. They are the only roses that are red. If I knew the Latin for red I would say it, if the Latin for rose, I would say it, the Latin for the only red in the oldest rose, I would say it. Were I Ovid, I would give you a rose and say that it is given for your eyes. I would take it, she says. I am glad you would, I say, touching her foot with my foot. Sassetta's rose, Pablo's rose.

Madame Matisse is a gentian, she says, touching my foot with her foot. Are all women flowers, all girls? Henri Rousseau was married to a sunflower, Cézanne to a pear tree.

Alice, I say. Yes, General Grant, she says. Pickaninny, I say. Augustus Caesar, she says. Do you see those pines over there, the ones that look like William McKinley addressing the Republican Party? You mustn't mention McKinley to Pablo, she says, he thinks he has trod on the honor of Spain. He has, I say, that is the American way. But the pines, Alice, the pines. I see them, she says, they have had a hard life. Do you, I say, see the bronze fall of needles beneath them, and know the perfume of rosin and dust and old earth we would smell if we climbed there? The flutter has begun, she says. And now look at the rocks, the cubist rocks, down the hills from the pines, and the red tile of the roofs, and the chickens in the yard there, the baskets. I see all that, she says. And having seen it, Alice? I ask. It is there to see, she says. That is the answer, I say. It is also the question.

MAO SAT in his red armchair looking benign and amused. Richard Nixon sank too far into his chair, his elbows as high as his ears. He beamed. He did not see the stacks of journals, the shelves packed with books, the bundles of folders, the writing brushes in jars. He beamed at Mao and at Dr. Kissinger, whom Mao had called a modern Metternich. The reporters had written that down.

The cluttered room was dark. What light there was came from tall windows which gave onto a courtyard as bleak as the playground of a grammar school. The translator said that Chairman Mao had asked about hegemony.

— We're for it, Richard Nixon said.

— Your aides are very young, Chairman Mao said.

— Are they? Richard Nixon asked.

— We must learn from you on that point, Chairman Mao said. Our government is all of old men.

Richard Nixon did not know what to say.

— Old, Chairman Mao said, but here, still here.

— The world is watching us, Richard Nixon said.

— You mean Taiwan, Chairman Mao said.

— No, Richard Nixon said, beaming, the world out there, the whole world. They are watching their TV sets.

Chairman Mao grinned and leaned back in his comfortable armchair.

— Ah so, he said, the world.

C. Musonius Rufus

IACTURA VIGORIS non fortuita est: agitur semper unum antitetrahedron. This dust of poppy, fitchet, bone is in an exact precession with which the gods are intimate but not our rough minds. Who, seeing a mother on her knees before the mammillaria of Cybebe, the Arvals flouring a calf for the knife, the standards of Quirinus in white mist around the watchfires, could believe that the gods are as indifferent as gravity? I huddle upon the wild rose, wait with the moth upon the wall, still as time.

All at first was the fremitus of things, the jigget of gnats, drum of the blood, fidget of leaves, shiver of light, boom of the wind. The tremor of my cry may have had something to do with choosing this threshold. There are other sills, empty places with intolerable glare, presences, noon quiet, lonely desperate desert wastes. I have died again in them. Those who go to the inhuman to place their hopes upon its alien rhythms, its bitter familiarity with nothing, its constant retreat from all that we can love, are hostages to vastation.

The majesty of the eagles in their gold, the arms raised in salute, the cries of obeisance, praise, and glory, the rise of the horns falling in fioritura: we never ask why the gods do not march in pomps, under arch after arch after arch.

I AM THE EMPEROR Balbinus kept in a jug. Together with Illyrian dust. Some flower petals a congenital mourner threw on the body are also in here along with a dead bee that was by occupation connected with the flowers.

The ghosts of bees I am told by the Consiliarii form a congrega-
tion in Cyprus though many are in Elysion itself and others where
they sang and foraged in their little lives. Hymettos and Chios
and such bright places.

Having been an emperor I am divine. Not the kin of the gods
as I had supposed but a god patent and absolute.

Nature is here too. In the first weeks when I was still drunk
with death I fretted to be out. An instinct as it were to flow was
my initial response to the new state of things. They had come to
me, crowding against the outside of the urn, the Consiliarii as
they called themselves, and hailed me as a divinity, just as the
general, the few senators, and functionaries recently hailed me
Imperator, anxiously, with not more than two *aves* apiece, immediately urging me make haste and flee. A rival faction in
Hispania or the Provincia Gallicum had also wrapped an emperor in the purple.

Trumpets, a roll of the drums, a hasty salute, and I was off.
We rode toward a forest.

The horror of the knives was soon over, and they talked of other
things while they were doing it. I remember squealing like a pig.

Light through matter makes it spin. Knowledge is to the mind
what water is to grime and sweat. I was turning in my jug and I
wanted to know why. No sooner had I wondered than I knew.
A Consiliarius put his face to mine, eye to eye. He turned as I
turned. A kind of red music ran in and out of my ears, what used
to be my ears.

Was I to spin forever, a *turbo* from which God himself had
whipped the cord? To ponder is to pose, and my answer was that
to turn is to exist. The very pollen which a bee has kicked from
the nectary of a poppy goes into orbit before it sifts down to
turn with the earth itself. A cow munching clover is pitching
forward with the large roll of the earth.

As the giddiness became usual, I longed to flock to what I
loved. My goats, for instance. My fig tree. My favorite window
looking out over the olives. Especially my goats. I saw their oblong
eyes and ellipsoid udders and cornered anatomies.

Was memory to bodger or enrich eternity? I remembered bar-
racks, parades, charges, hospitals, speeches, but as a mouse over-
hears the talk of a room from the rafters, with perfect unconcern.

What is there to shiver so when a flight of sparrows flutters through my middle? I am not flesh. Unbroken habit of flinching where the body used to be will no doubt fade in time. If I am in time. I think I have become a globe, like all things that spin. Light is round. The Consiliarii have taught me that. It goes in all directions at once and thus balloons out from its source. Spirit must be a substance very like light. Old polarity of head and butt no longer maintains. I find that it is sweet to flow through water. Is this thirst?

I say flow and flit and other words of motion without knowing what I mean. For I do not leave my jug. Here in this dark I can still see the pitted terra-cotta interior. The dead bee. Withered flowers. The bee is on its back with its little legs bent at the knees. But I also see an army crossing a ford, a vineyard, and barbarians on mares. Their slant eyes glint like blue steel. Their hair is combed down over their faces and tucked into their belts in front. Gold clasps hold the hair away from their faces. The hair of the head is combed into the hair of the beard. They stink of tallow and horse.

I see flax and roses as if the jelly of the eye were amber honey from Illyria. Whatever I have for an eye it is never closed. Lids are flesh. The eye was spirit all along. Imagine that if you can, whoever beyond the Consiliarii can feel my thoughts. And I can smell. That was spirit too. O, and I can feel. Not surfaces. It takes two for an encounter and I am nothing. But I can pass through. In a tree I feel the thousand threads of water that rise from the roots to the leaves.

I move constrained by the shape of my jar in a kind of crouch, my elbows on my knees, my knees on a line with my ears. Weightless, I still adhere to the ground. At first I waddled through the leaves of trees but found such progress absurd. I went up toward the clouds. O Hercules, what loneliness, what devastation, what fear! I like the open road, especially stationing myself on a bridge. I try to talk to donkeys, not knowing what to say.

Nor is it congenial to go downward into the earth. I first ventured a well. Then I went down to where iron grows. Down past root seines in loam like condered oakgall and down past yellow marl hard with quartz the splintered ores begin. Green, edged, with the black metal smell horses hate and wine sours next to, and which thunder has entered. Chill, sacred iron, bitter with lightning. Stay away. It is not human. It is from the beyond, from up, the stuff of the moon and cold stars. It is down, the pit is iron. It neither breathes nor moves. The gods own it but it is not a god. Pity is not in it.

I have thrust myself into a sunflower and washed in its basil green. Near deep iron I have shuddered and gone numb.

Like a snake I take my warmth from the world. I make none of my own. This godstuff I'm of is not by Hercules flesh. It is a kind of air, but more organized and articulate. There is the ghost of a bunion on the ball of my left foot, the soldier's corn, where we pivot. Though I feel, there is no seriousness to it, as in a dream. The ride of a wasp through my eyes, rain through my arms, wheat awns combing my bowels, all I meet in my flow swims through me as easily as a fish.

But things do not always get to me or I to them. I stream across geese to a wall and find myself in a country I have never seen, the brick hives of Chaldea mayhap, Indus fowls bright as flowers in the streets.

I nod in a cowstall, liking the straw and dried pease. I wake by a river, near a skiff, an old Tiber herm brown with time, baskets. I exist without continuity. While squatting in a wine vat I am suddenly on board the *Hecate* sailing for Marsala. And in my urn all the while.

We are digging a canal across Greece, through rock, the depth of a mountain's height.

If you have never swung a pickaxe, brother, never been chained ankle to ankle, you know no more than a child what's ahead of you.

The canal is to connect the bay of Corinth and the Saronicus and be a path from the Adriatic to the Ionian. God knows when they began it, some centuries ago judging by my first look, and Rome will be as old as the world itself when it is finished, if it is finished.

Greece! I would have taken this place to be Africa. Corinth is somewhere over there, they say, a separate city from the Acrocorinth, on a hill, sacred to the slut Aphrodite. .

Flies, shit, sweat rancid as a whiff of billy goat, fatigue as deep in the bone as water in the sea.

There is a kind of exhilaration in having lost all, once the anguish subsides. Once the anguish subsides.

We are chained ankle to ankle, and to each other. My fellow to the left is a Scythian who lives off fury. He eats his beans like a wolf, he scoops clay when he can get at it and eats that too. He prays to strange gods.

My fellow to the right is Roman enough, but dead. I tell him that they have our bodies only, not our souls, but he stares at me as if I were a lunatic.

To want nothing, I tell him, is freedom, to will nothing is death. He wills nothing. He wants his freedom, still, and his soul is sick with that lust. It is a terrible want that adds to the weight of the pick, thickens fatigue, mixes rage with mere despair.

We sleep in our filth, unconscious as soon as they order us to lie down. And we rise while we are still asleep, and drink swill, and go off under the lashes to the rockface. It takes them awhile to unchain the dead, and it is harder on us, in both spirit and body, to drag a corpse in the chains. Yesterday we dragged poor Mnescus half the morning before the crew with the files and snippers could get around to us.

The third or fourth swing of the pick and he died standing, his tongue out like a mouthful of sponge, his eyes rolled back white, his old knees trembling like a wet dog.

After you've had your fill of horrors, they cease to burn. There is to be nothing else, after all. It rains, we work in mud. We are grateful for the difference. The beans are sometimes black rather than red. New prisoners arrive, and we are avid to learn why they are here.

The horns, the long horns blare, and we are off in our chains, morning after morning. Yeorgi, three down to the left, will probably die before the day is out. I've looked my look at the son of a bitch of a guard when they had us out at the crack of dawn, meaning that if he had the featherweight of a man in him, he would take Yeorgi out of the gang, spitting blood as he was, fever in his eyes.

The guidons were up, no man might speak. The horns, the old sergeants who had frozen their balls on the Rhine and roasted them in the Oxus held their dignity under the standards, the drums, and the shouting in our faces, as if we were barbary apes, the shit in the latrines being shoveled over, another day, another day.

They even have an *emperor* here, as if we were the army on a campaign, or a deputation in Hispania. It is the old fart himself, a marble bust thereof, around which they put the purple night-shirt, and a breastplate and greaves. They march him behind the SPQR, goose-stepping and pounding on the drums, jingling the sistrum, and roaring *Ave!*

O to kiss a pig's butt and it ripe with diarrhea!

Once when I was in Old Granny's Pisspot, that windowless judgment down by the Maxima, black as Egypt on a Thursday night, a wealth of rats traveling in all directions, jugged all over again because the monster's spies had found another nest of philosophers and stirred us up with their sticks and frogmarched us before a hogjowled magistrate who sentenced us from behind his nosegay, looking at us sideways, to three months' darkness, or longer, subject to the emperor's *pleasure*, once when I was going fishbelly white and blind as a mole because the emperor emits little yipes of horror when he hears of a philosopher in Rome, a letter came to me from God knows where or how, it was tossed in with the mildewed bilge they fed us.

A letter! It was from Apollonius.

Esteemed Musonius, it said, it was written in Greek. Esteemed Musonius, than whom no one is more able in philosophy, my heart in sore pressed to learn that you are detained by the government. And so on and so forth, and he would come to see me.

The next handing around of the slop I asked the guard if his imperial majesty's postal service, famed for its delivery of eclogues from the Caucasus to Celtiberia and of sycophantic procurators' lies from the Pillars of Hercules to the spice groves of Arabia Felix, extended to this colicky whore's ass of a jail?

— He is here, he whispered.

— *He?* Who?

— The wizard.

— Apollonius?

— Him.

— *Me hercle, nai gonades kynoi!*

And then there was a scratching about in the dark, and the slit of gray light up the corridor that one saw when the guards slipped in and out opened up into a rectangle of glare, and light even got into my cell, strange as snow in the desert.

I could see him in black outline only, legs as spindly as a stork's, nose huge, dressed in some antique robe with fringes, something one's Etruscan maiden aunt would turn up in at the Circus.

— Musonius?

— The wretch himself.

I should not have replied in despair, for it is more painful to the free to see you jailed than it is to be jailed.

— Menippus here.

Menippus? He was, like Damis, one of the master's henchmen. He wanted to make a trial run, he said, before he brought the Philosopher. Meanwhile, he had brought another letter, which I read by the light of the open door up the passage.

Apollonius the learner to Musonius the philosopher, greeting! I would like to come share your lodgings in order that I might share your conversation, it said, so help me Jupiter and Hera. Unless, it went on, you cannot believe that Herakles freed Theseus from the dreary house of Hades. Answer, dear soul, what you would have me do. *Erróso.*

— I shall take your answer down, Menippus hissed at me in the half dark.

I dictated, his stylus flicked at the wax.

I said that he was not to come. I could see Nero having the hysterica passio into a perfumed handkerchief at the report that the most spiritual of philosophers, the stringy haired, barefoot ascetic Apollonius had moved into a jail cell with the red Rufus. I can defend myself, I said. My mind is stronger than ever. I have done no wrong. Find my students and talk with them, until we can converse in the quiet and peace befitting philosophy. I said that to fit in with what I knew to be his style. He knew that like randy old Socrates I could talk philosophy in stables and at the baths, in the fish market and on the road, practically anywhere except at a rich man's table, where the level of conversation is below that of a dovecote of whores conniving to up their prices.

He would never find the cobbler who was one of my best disciples, old Marcus who had a true flare for the Pythagorean poetry of things and a noble grasp of stoic wisdom. Nor would he stumble upon the Senator who keeps his philosophy to himself, or the slavewoman Dorcas whose dignity of mind I would place beside that of Cicero. More than likely he would ferret out, such is my luck, the scamp Fabricius who follows me for my knuckly rhetoric, as he calls it, and who spends half his time at the gymnasia ogling backsides and pretty eyes and the other half pumping his seed onto the garret ceiling or alley walls or tiles of the public baths. But the boy has a mind and a lovely imagination, and Apollonius probably has the Platonic flare for a snub nose and black curls and a peplon that stops in the middle of the butt. And when Nero throws Fabricius in the jug, he'll take it like a man.

Aie! Apollonius, Apollonius.

He wrote again. He reminded me that Socrates, refusing help from his friends, was executed.

I wrote back that Socrates died because he would not take the trouble to defend himself. I shall defend myself.

Errôso.

He has since learned for himself what the inside of a Roman prison is like. Pythagoreans and Stoics are all one to the imperial police.

Roma, you old baggage and suet sack, you are worthy of your Nero.

A DELEGATION CAME of trembling splendor, Consuls of the dead they said they were. One lifted a hand. Their patrician faces and beautiful feet seemed to me to be godlike, their eyes a fidget of light.

— We are the wardens, they said.

I confused them with the other delegation, the colonels of the Praetoria who came to make me emperor. On both occasions a dread chill struck my bones, my real bones the first time, a memory of bones the second. Great moments should not have made me feel so small. But the letter of the law is spite. I have had ample opportunity to see that with awful certainty. The law requires an emperor. The great families had no more emperors. The landlords and the equestrians declined absolutely, having better sense. Anybody would do. When great nations go to seed, you will find all sorts of men in the purple, provincial tax collectors, lawyers, bald generals with remote victories in the Rhineland to their credit, grocers, and petty army officials, like me.

To the Consiliarius with silver eyes who sat with a basket of anemones as red as blood at his elbow I said I had been made emperor of Rome a fine morning in Pannonia. By noon we were crossing the Ister, where I was advised to flee toward Singidunum with a contingent of Praetoriani. At sunset they abandoned me.

Surely I was not the first emperor to pee the purple? I remember banked rack over the Carpathians, a band of Gypsies, a brown child riding a goat. I gave the Gypsies the damp toga and six denarii in exchange for an ass on which I made my way into a terrible wood. I soon heard hooves and saw the knives in the half light. Never should man kill anything at all.

If the name Balbinus does not go into your ear like Caligula or Augustus it is because history is a slut. She will accept pomp everytime over worth. Did not Augustus say with the last of his breath that instead of a funeral oration he wanted a round of applause?

It is because the historians would find little beyond my name to record that the Consiliarii were patient with me. They seemed not to want to obtrude, and kept a polite distance when they appeared. Of one I could make out a blue eye only. The rest was shadow. The second was clearer, the folds of his toga fell through a rose bush, a very pretty pattern.

Another time they came through an ilex with a rabbit in each hand. A sacrifice, I assumed. One that I had perhaps omitted on the outside, the inside, whichever I'm on now. I can't get it straight. Pensum is verbum in this layer of the world, between the tissue of light and its stay on the bought and hollow of things. They are of our realm, I understood them to mean. We may talk with eyes here, I don't know. And the pensum inside the word folds out here. I was beholden to these staring bucks. Even they come through the membrane, the one said to the other, meaning me.

I began to see the significance of having come across with the bee. It brought me, I think.

I found a Consiliarius in a stand of thistle by a milestone, turning himself leisurely inside out and back again, like candlesmoke in a still room.

— Jupiter! I said, remembering that I had not thought to ask after the gods.

He closed his hand and opened it.

— Jupiter, he said.

— Juno?

He joined his hands.

I gave it up. I knew that he would make a fist for Mars and a finger for Venus, would knit his knuckles for Minarva and smooth his hand along the air for Mercurius.

— Themselves! I cried. I am not a schoolboy.

He went into the milestone like water into sand.

ROMA, ROMA. Pain makes us all equal here, in Rome it is the differentiator. We have had to learn not to laugh at the bloody stump, the epileptic jerking along, the milky eye, the legless. Such amusements belong to the city, where a lady, her face a glory of powder, Sidonian lips, a tower of hair woven with pearls, earrings like stars, can shake her litter with a fit of laughter at the sight of a humpback swinging along on crutches, where mothers, barristers, doctors gasp with pleasure as two dwarves hack themselves to a butchered ruin in the Circus.

Of the crucifixions, that peculiarly Roman entertainment, a Greek said to me one day in tears, *have you no Goddess of mercy?* None, I said. He had seen a crucifixion against his will, and had been held by the horror of it longer than he could stand, were he sane at the time, as he said, for he lost his mind when he realized that the spectators were *laughing.*

And yet he had not seen, as I have, a thief almost apologetic for having such a terrible time with his pain as the nails were driven into his wrists and feet. He bellowed like a bull, driven wild by the pain, and when they pulled the *crux* up to go into its socket his scream pierced to the quick of your bones, but you could scarcely hear it over the laughter of the audience.

Here we do not laugh at pain, our lot in common. We have only averted eyes or a word of courage to serve for compassion, having learned something of what the Greeks mean by sympathy. Or is it shame?

The Procurator comes down in a litter to the channel, a

Garamantian trotting beside him with an umbraculum. A wart tarantulous and inauspicious sprouted from the flange of the old custus's nose and a goiter the size of a piglet wrenched his chin around to his shoulder. He kept shouting that he must not be brought near any lepers.

The SPQR rides high before, carried by a wheezing corporal whose leather cinctures squeak and whose face shines with sweat.

The Procurator wiggles his ringed fingers at a scribe. The Machinator leans to listen. The litter out among the ravaged earth which we are hacking and loading into buckets looks like nothing so much as a beribboned and curtained cradle that has been spirited from a censorial nursery onto the wastes of Calabria.

We see a tall soldier from the guard summoned to the custator's frilly lecticula. The old boy swings out. He needs to piss and it is his whim to piss against the soldier, who stands at attention while he is being pissed upon. There is natural philosophy in us all. I hope he did not take it as an honor, knowing all the while that he did.

I SKIDDLE DOWN into grass fading to hay, grass bearding out into awns, worts, burrs, and docks, down among hoppers and midges sawing the air, tumblebugs, ants, and silvery crawlers. I find a ball of grass, a nest, and there lies a mama mouse with three implausibly small and exact baby mice at her teats, pumping with their paws. Her belly, throat, and whiskers are white, otherwise she is as brown as an acorn except for her eyes, which are like wet black apple seeds. She is patient and alert. Her tail lies across her young like the pin of a fibula.

O Lady Mouse, I breathe, your well wisher here who has come to visit, the round of nothing before you in this fine grass, was the emperor of Rome.

Whereupon the Consiliarii were suddenly with me, one with a red moth for an eye, a sycamore seed for another, mulberry leaves for hair. Clustered bees were his beard, a lion's bones, still joined, his body, a lizard his sex. His fellow was a leopard through which you could see, like water.

— Mus mater haec, Moth Eye said. Here in this place a temple used to stand. The ground is still sacred.

Whose temple? I watched the mouse no bigger than a thumb and her brood snuggled so neatly between her forelegs and hindlegs, eager little fellows.

— Diktynna, Leopard answered, the Lady. Cut stone is not to her liking, and she abides these long houses with their thin rock trees out of the courtesy of the undying until old Kelp Beard knocks them down, at which we have heard her laugh, her and her girls, her and her bears.

Am I now her kin? Does my divinity put me into her family?

— O no, Moth Eye was quick to say, too quick, for I am easily confused. The gods, he went on, are powers like wind and snow, mercy and light. You, an emperor, when you find something to care for, will be given the necessary power to care for it. That will be the extent of your godhood. There is a king from the north who rides with wrens and spells them on their eggs, an earl of the Angles who roosts with gannets, a queen of the Belgii who has lived for a hundred years with spotted toads in the great wood that grows between the Rhenus and the Mosa.

THEY MOUNT the crosses where we can see them if we lift our eyes from our pickaxes, carrion crows crowded along the arms.

Distance, distance. I can lie at night in the stink of piss and smegma and regain the window in which I sat at Poplicola's house on the Via Nola, English geese gabbling among the poultry for a pastoral note, the cool house warmed by our yellow Roman light that filled the windows like a kindness, a din of traffic beyond just enough garden walls to make a pleasant patter, like rain, or the womenfolk in the atrium.

I remember my young head turned by the idea of worth, and my book, an Antisthenes or Hekaton, with the life of Cleanthes of Assos in it, Zeno's successor in the Stoa.

A man worthy of carrying on for Zeno! Zeno, who had died at a full old age by simply ceasing to eat. He was in pain toward the end. *Quit nagging*, he cried out to death, *can't you see that I'm coming of my own accord?*

Cleanthes, my book told, was a boxer who had heard of philosophy and came to Athens with but four small coins in his mouth. Zeno accepted him as a pupil. He made his living as a water drawer and miller, selling water for gardens by night and crushing meal at kitchen doors.

O the strangeness of Athens three hundred years ago! So hale was Cleanthes that he was brought before the Areopagitas and asked how he made his living, for he seemed to do nothing but walk up and down the Stoa with Zeno and his barefoot flock, talking about time and necessity, evil and the moon. When witnesses testified that he was their water carrier and their meal grinder, the archons voted him an income of ten minas, which, on the advice of Zeno, he refused.

I began to fall in with the stoics then and there, behind the followers of the followers of Cleanthes.

The mockers twitted him for toting buckets of water. This, they brayed, is philosophy? I know the oily slide of their eyes upward, the ringed hand hanging limp from the wrist, the urine and garlic rictus of ape's teeth and the lizard tongues playing with the money in their mouths.

Do I, Cleanthiskos carissimus would reply with the true Zenonian gall, only hustle buckets? You've missed me chopping weeds? Watering lettuce, basil, melons? O, but I *slave* at philosophy, dear citizens!

One day he showed around a handful of coins. See, he said, I could support a second Cleanthes were I two of myself. Life in the streets of Athens was a kind of myth.

That old Etruscan olive elf and her hoot owl must have had occasions when she wondered why the Greeks built her a city. Homely old Minarva! *Ignea rima micans*, with a farmer's rude understanding of that *rima*, thundery old maiden aunt with her bundles of lightning, an owl witch that these Greeks in their paganry have tried to make into a lady.

He was a slow learner, Cleanthes, and never quite understood the physics of Zeno. Yet he studied harder than any of Zeno's students. The wags called him Herakles, meaning that he was all brawn and skimpy on brains.

He became popular in a way that usually worked with the Athenians. He wore nothing under his cloak, and one windy day when he was walking with his adolescent followers to some rite on the Acropolis a gust opened his clothes. The streets were full of people who applauded his handsome body and talked about it for days. Thereafter he was treated with deference and respect.

Still, he was the butt of Zeno's collegium, the ass who chose the hardest work, a man proud of his poverty. He said that he would rather dig rock than have to amuse himself. Meaning the rich. Accused of being afraid to botch a task, he replied that this was why he always did things right.

Sositheos included a joke about Cleanthes in a mimiambus at the theater, and Cleanthes did not so much as bat an eye at the insult. The audience of course looked at him as much as at the actor Sositheos. No rage, no blush. Seeing nothing but nobility, they rose in their seats and clapped for Cleanthes. Then they threw cucumbers and sandals at Sositheos until he fled the stage.

I ROLL INTO a hawthorn all white and green, around which I fit like a bubble. A sparrow and my knee occupy the same fragrant space wreathed with blossoms, a bee and my right eye. The ground beneath is so intimate, so congenial, that I consider staying here for the life of the bush, to feel rain, wind, snow. Part of me go off to be honey, part wither and fall. In my shoulder the sparrow would weave her nest, feed her young, straddle them with stretched wings atremble in rain, cry other birds away.

The Consiliarii came to me through a light busy with points of fire.

— Accident, they said, is design.

I turned in my jug like the slow spin of milk in a churn.

— Here, they said, the bobbin is unwound, the engines of futility dismantled and laid out, so that one could see what rain on a Tuesday had to do with the nightmare of a Spanish cook, how a lie told in the reign of Antoninus caused a Scot to lead a life of total illusion.

WE SPREAD OUT in a line, defined by our chains, and dig. The line behind us gathers the rubble of our digging into baskets. Between the lines the sergeants move with their whips. The senate drones on, the armies at the borders of the empire stick the Celts and Huns like so many wild boars, and in the Circus hungry lions claw the bowels out of screaming Iudaei while the Emperor God picks his nose.

Once you have muscles in the shoulders and arms, the pick work is not so murderous. And good thick calluses.

Brother, I say to the Sicilian they have chained to my right leg, what brings you to the *inferi* before your time?

Quidnam, ha! Quoquo, ha!

Tears welled up in his eyes.

— *Uxorem necatu' misellam.* He sank the pickaxe so deep into the rock that he had to fight it out again.

— *Puggiunculo!*

Vae! All the crimes of these wretches look like mine, and all their faces are mirrors. I almost said to him that I too had killed my wife, though I have yet to learn whether I have or not. It little matters whether we cut the fool as a hissing miser, farting tyrant, slave, usurer, madman, whore, or pigherd. By playing the philosopher I have given a good woman more grief than any simple soul ought to face.

I taught her to read and write, true, and showed her how the philosophical mind has other pleasures and pains than the blind herd and the dreaming rich. I freed her from superstition until she could hear the raven caw and laugh at it as of no matter. We even kept a pet owl to show that we were immune from the paralysis of ignorant fear. She made herself pet it, though it looked as malevolent as a baby gorgon, and in the night she cried out *Surely we shall all die!*

But I must live with the look on her face the first time they took me away.

The first arrest and sentence, from which I came back. *I came back.* That is the reason I can endure this shit. Not the hope that some sane man will slit the rotten old Catmit's wezand from ear to ear, or that an honest praetor will lower his hemorrhoids onto a bench free of the fingersnap of a politician, or that Iustitia will flounce down from the clouds swinging her ensis and libra, but the fact that I have been to the bottom and walked up again keeps me swinging my pick.

We go down into the earth as we dig, and the sky becomes a bay of blue above us. I read the symbol, I take the measure of the calamity.

IN SPILLWAYS of light through leaves I see boys playing with staves. A black bird with Scythian beak blocks my view. But I see that I can see through that fowl, see sunlight in its bones, the sky through its feathers, see boys through boys, trees through a wall, and on and on until what I see is a trash of color, beautiful rubble.

There are days when I see only white everywhere.

Days when I can hear nothing, see nothing, feel nothing. I am loneliest then, and fearful. I have learned to search the white for a yellow dot, which grows if I stare at it, until a gnat-swarm of bilious specks gathers around it and becomes a detail: a horse's eye, a jug of olive oil, a whetstone.

Once the yellow spot became a fire, thorns cracking under a pot, which emerged from the white after a long wait. I looked, for patience is sometimes all I have, until there were barbarians sitting around the pot. Their eyes were handsome, strange, intelligent. Their women suckled infants at fine brown breasts. Yellow dogs sat on their haunches and grinned.

There was a moon, later, and even later, an owl, their god.

I was going to float among them when the Consiliarii came to me, quickly, like lighting birds in an opposing wind, and said, *No,* that I could not consort with the barbarians.

They said their name, a word with too many syllables and with the accent impossibly on the penultimate. He was a commander of weather and water, their god. His brother is a snake. He is pleased by drums. By bells, gongs, chants.

Firelight on the grease of their cheeks kept me ahover just beyond their gray horses, and the beautiful *chink chink* of their kanoon by which the womenfolk sang lullabies to their young.

Their time is not yours, the Consiliarii said as they shooed me back.

— Give me, then, I said, my bee! My sponsor across the Styx. My evangelical bee.

They smiled, the tall Consiliarii. Where we were rose with a jolt, tilted, and shot forward. A music as of birds and laughing children went with us, though measured like a Lydian dance.

And on that silver line between the brown earth and the blue deep of the sky, in a field of clover red and green the whole horizon across, we came to my bee.

— O golden-thighed mite! I cried.

— Wax hexagon! said the bee. Right deflection under azimuth, earthspin downward polaroid greens in quanta red shift, dip and shake, forward zoom.

— Brother! I said.

— A shake and a shake, it sang. Angle, angle! Citron ginger sugar green.

— Brother!

— Buzz off, Onion Bulb, it said. Go jump in your jug.

THE FIRST TIME they got in their rabbit brains that we were magicians I was sentenced to an island. We worked the oars going out, we arrived so glad to be rid of the sea and the whip that we scarcely asked what our punishment was to be. Labor, we assumed, a bitter existence we assumed, the life of a slave.

But there was no garrison there, no master of the whip. Nothing. Rock, bushes, weeds, and the winking glare of the sea all around.

And no water. We looked, the miserable lot of us. *There was no water on the island.*

We were murderous pimps, men who had lost all to the *exactors'* moneylenders, one-handed thieves, highwaymen, merchants of children, *magi*, philosophers.

Here in the Great Corinthian Ditch we at least know we shall have our swill, and even when. It's a kind of frog spawn with iron beans. But it is always there.

Discipline is our Orcus and our salvation. Rome itself is a shapeless bundle of shitten pissburnt sweatscalded bubonic rotten rags held together with a bronze wire of discipline. Our Centurio gets drunk every sixth day, you can tell by the silly smile and the cinculus on backwards. Every Ides the Dux puts on his yellow frock and goes off with the sergeants and corporals to their Mithraeum they have here in the wilderness. They call each other Brother Lion and Brother Crow.

Even I am here by law. I am a wizard.

The catchpoll described me to the Magistrate when I was hauled in on the charge that landed me here as a subverter of the laws of the State and a blasphemer against the gods.

— Crap, I said.

— What? said the Magistrate.

— Crap, your Honor. *Merda.*

The Accusator read from the charge: Teaches that women are the equal of men and that their status as infants in the adoption of their husbands is pernicious and against nature. Advocates that women should be educated. Teaches that the gladiators are inhuman and that the spectators at the Circus are bestial and coarse of mind, including his Divinity the Emperor. That taxes are collected by usurers, who keep half, that Roman history is largely fiction, that few barbarian peoples have ever exhibited such moral degradation as the Roman mob, that the Roman gentry are more firmly enslaved to their vices than their slaves to their bondage . . .

He read on, and on, flicking his tongue across his teeth at the items he considered scandalous and raising his eyebrows at the parts clearly definable as sedition.

— To whom, the Magistrate thought to ask, were these *ridicularia* being taught?

A shuffle of tablets, and a list held up, as if by this token damnation was sealed.

— Clavis, a cobbler, Passer, a catamite, Hispana, a bawd, Tacita, an old woman who keeps a goat, Virga, another catamite, Modestus, a slave, Minicius, a poet . . .

— Scum.

— *Vero.*

— Why do you do this? the Magistrate said to me, with no uncertainty that my perversity was not as clear to me as it was to him.

— To teach men what is in their power to control and what isn't, so that they may cultivate their character and make a garden of their soul.

My failure is to address men as if they were classrooms.

The Magistrate rearranged his chins, milked the lobe of an ear, and asked how many offenses I had committed against the Roman Senate and People.

— Five times jailed and once exiled, the Recorder recited. All for sedition. Repeatedly reprimanded for conducting *sessiuncula philosophica,* so called, to no purpose, as the accused is pigheaded.

So they sent me to Corinth to dig a canal through solid rock from this bay of the ocean to that bay of the ocean.

In my time the world was mad.

CONSIDER GLAUKOS, the Consiliarii said together, who fell into a jar of honey as he chased a mouse, and drowned. I saw the consonance of image with image, his jar and mine, the honey in his, the bee in mine. But I was bald and fat, briefest of emperors. Glaukos, they smiled, was a little boy, his hair coppery and finished, neat cross his forehead and snug around his ears. His limbs were so kin in color to the honey in which he fell that the first astonished eyes thought that only his shirt was what they saw.

At first they did not know where he was. Minos sent for men of second sight, and for the godly Kyretes, the circle dancers who could claim the ear of Zeus. They came, they danced, they beat their swords on their shields.

There is a cow among your herds, they said, that changes color twice a day, every fourth hour. The morning finds it white, noon red, evening black. Who knows that cow can bring your son to life when he is found.

That cow, the seer Polyidos said to Minos, is like a mulberry, which is first white, then red, then black.

So hasten, said Minos, who knew by the look in his eye that Polyidos could find his son.

And find Glaukos he did. He knew the jar as soon as he saw it. And none too soon, for a snake had found it just before and was coiled around the jar, sliding upward, as if it were an arm of the octopus painted there in blue.

Polyidos killed the snake with a stone. It came loose from the jar like a knot untied and lay limp in the dust. But before Polyidos could draw near, a second snake rode forward. It smelled its fellow with its tongue, slid away as quickly as a fish through water, and came back with the leaf of an herb in its mouth before Polyidos could take two steps toward the jar. It stuffed the leaf in the dead snake's mouth, and waited. Before long, the dead snake raised its head, shivered down its length, and drew itself together to move.

And with that same herb, said one Consiliarius, Polyidos revived the drowned Glaukos and returned him to his father.

You are like the child Glaukos, said the other, drowned in the honey of time. We think a snake will come to be your dream. Our sources are confused. We are only messengers.

Rɪsᴇ ᴜᴘ, dead man, help me drive my row! Grieve, Rufus, I nagged myself with my philosophy, for the poverty of the rich, the impotence of the powerful. The discontinuous ownership of what cannot be kept has smashed us all to shards, the love of what cannot be loved has changed our minds until the business of mind is a ewe in the thicket. Man will die weary of what he was never intended to do.

The ecliptic had left the Ram, where every dawn from Theseus to Tiberius the sun rose red, bringing rain and heron on the one equinox, silencing cricket and scythe on the other, the time of the bloody Persephone and the sleep of snakes, but the world itself was mad.

The Fish were as they have been through eternity, swimming in their forked river and with their field of starry wheat between them, but the world was made.

Men with ulcers for eyes carry baskets of rock up the face of the excavation. They are chained, they will not go astray. Hernias bound up with rags brown with urine, piles, teeth rotting with the ache of death itself, boils, welts splitting green, jaundice, fever, hair alive with lice: they ought to bring the Roman crowd here to see us.

They could build a grandstand and bring the spectators here in excursion boats. The slaves at the oars would serve for the praeludium. No doubt they would find it boring. They have become bored with the chariot races, and they have long since ceased to see horses, at whose deaths they begin to flutter their fans and gossip.

Your Roman has in fact never quite seen anything but the surface, the outside of anything. He would die of shame to be a slave because he would be *seen* as a slave. You might know that Roman sovereignty would be inherent in a color. And no Roman would be seen watching the butcher work in the Circus except in the whitest of togas.

God bless the flies! Their maggots are our only doctors.

The spectators would much rather have seen us on the island, the waterless island.

— *Nonnunquam pluit, nonne?*

— Never. It has not rained in these islands since the dawn of the world.

Were it to rain, we considered, we could let it drench our clothes and wring them over our mouths. Was there dew? Could we dig a well? And with what?

Thirst is a deprivation that drives you mad before it kills you. I knew that much.

There is a man here in the gangs at Corinth whom madness has touched to the marrow. We go stupid as we are worked to death, drained of the last of our mother wit, humanity out, dullness in. Madness, though, is a kind of conflagration of the intellect, a man locked in a room beating on all the doors and walls just in case somthing might give. It is childish, madness, the irrational frenzy of wanting. Yet to a dullard who has long since absorbed his childhood with greed, the bondage of easily gratified desires, the return of a smidgin of innocence shocks him into madness. A man rots when the child in him dies.

The *genius* philosophers urge us to heed is but a grasp of one's childhood, any moment of which unrelinquished to the demons of time is sufficient to keep the god Apollo near enough, near enough. One touch of virginity can sweeten the sourest vinegar of a ravaged soul, one touch of liberty still green, one unforgotten chill at looking at a moth on the back of the hand. Savage folly in a turm of white butterflies, a quitch shot with crickets, hide and seek in the barley awns!

THISTLE, GOLDFINCH, STAR. A star in its eye, the goldfinch pecks a blue thistle with pert bill. Cricket chitter charms the air. Anna Perenna! sings the finch. Anna Perenna!

I am, or think I am. I know I was. I and the bee, we were. I and the bee and the flower. And now we all three are, somewhere. Of the jug I do not know the tenses. It was once on a potter's wheel and in a kiln, and before that it was clay, perhaps in a river. Some craftsman, the potter I suppose, has painted a horse on it, a kind of duck or goose, and some zigzags and stars. Has anything of mine survived? I signed my name over and over. I was never politician enough to kill my enemies, they are great sources of fame. My name must be in a list somewhere. Some schoolmaster will say my name to little boys on their benches.

I escaped a lot of the meanness of the world. I was not a slave or a tax collector.

My wife and her moustache all the depilatories however astringent could not remove rarely haunt my reveries, though I wonder sometimes with a memory as of the knives if she will ever join me here in the swirls of pollen between the two plies of the cloth of light that adheres to all the surfaces of the world. That is where I may be. It was always the outside of light I saw alive. I am most certainly now on the other side. The back of orange is brown. The back of yellow blue. But I may be between the outer and the inner film.

Sometimes when the campagna is hazy with wagon dust and twilight, rain clouds blackening in the north, I see lizards the size of elephants clumping through ferns as big as oaks. They go on their hind legs in a hopping glide, holding their forepaws out like women crossing the street. Their eyes are little and stupid, their tails as long as a ship. They gobble and honk.

I go into a nettle when I see them, peering out through the fuzz. I have mentioned them to the Consiliarii, who say they cannot see them, and praise me for my gifts, and question me as to what I mean by the word *size*. I have given up trying to explain. A dog is smaller than a horse, I tell them by way of illustration. They smile and look at each other in wonder.

OUR MADMAN has made himself a ragdoll from scraps of cloth, sticks, and bits of twine. He hangs it around his neck while we swing the picks, and cuddles it at night. His eyes are as lost as the exiles' eyes on the island where there was no water, eyes that were fearful of a bush, of the sun, of footsteps from behind.

What to a child is a tor blue in its own shadow as the light goes level but the humped house of the old steganopodous lar himself whose grin all grizzle and whose pounce *illotis manibus* are why there are hearths in the world at all?

Habitarunt di quoque silvas collesque. What elves are the gods
that we should forget to shiver when they crack a stick in the frost
outside the house? Children are not the wolves that men become,
if they had a grandmother worthy of the name.

I've admired the ragdoll of our madman, who watched me for
five *puncti* together, looking for the spite. He hid the doll in his
tatters, but next day he motioned me over with an idiot smile. He
was nursing the doll at his bosom.

— We must be so careful, I said.

— *Sice sicuti!* he sputtered, crouching to look sharply over his
shoulder.

I look into his eyes and know that madness is not the way I
shall go. I am damned to sanity and to hope. I have seen her
again whom I'd never hoped to see. I have seen wildflowers in the
wall after they put us on the waterless island to die as best we
could. Fortuna moves with fire in her left hand, water in her right.
Discovery is always more than what you meant to find. You look
for a woman to bake your bread and be delicious in your bed and
you find patience and kindness. You look for truth and find
strength. I looked for water and found C. Musonius Rufus. I lost
him, I think, in the galleys coming out, perhaps in the windowless
jail before. Perhaps I had never found him at all. The imitation of
a man who found Rufus spoke with the tongue of the shills and
panders around him, saw as they saw, lost hope as they lost hope,
threw hope away with the abandon of the self hater. Fortuna
was a whore, what doubt could there be of it? Cleanthes and Zeno!
Had they ever been closed in the bilge of a Roman galley, had
they been abandoned on a rock in the Aegean? They had never
seen human beings indistinguishable from the gutter rats of Rome.

We talked murder, to drink the blood. We armed ourselves
with sticks and rocks, making territories. I found an overhang of
rock that I could be under part of the day. The tide of our sea is
very shallow, but it was enough to fill my shelter.

In the part farthest back of this little inlet the sand was whiter,
finer. I thought how if I were a child I would delight in that clean
place under the rock, in the translucent green shelf of cool water
over the sand. Jagged stone in hand, I kept one eye on the rise
above me, one on the hollow. How long had I seen a burble in the

surface of the thin water where it slipped as shallow as papyrus over the sand?

IL RICORDO DELLE ANTICHE PROVE FREME NEI CUORI, COSÌ COME L'IMPETO VERSO IL FUTURO!

La Banda Municipale Filarmonica di Rapallo stood at parade rest in front of the flag of the Motherland, the standard of Genoa, and the *bandiera fascista*. An honor guard in black shirts, jackboots, and alpine hats stood behind the flags, carbines on the ready. The bandmaster mopped sweat from under his chin. For the fortieth time sometime had hushed their chatter and horseplay to say that they heard the automobiles.

— *Adesso!*

— *Finalmente!*

NON BISOGNA CREDERE E FAR CREDERE ALLA FACILITÀ DELLA GUERRA: SAREBBE UN ALIMENTARE DELLE ILLUSIONI ASSURDA. LA GUERRA SARÀ ASPRA E DURA.

The moment, if ever it would begin, was sacred and potent with glory. The Duce di Fascismo, himself, would arrive with certain members of the Party. He was to be greeted with *Giovanezza, Giovenezza!* They would salute in the salute of the Caesars, he would salute. The bandmaster would shout the order to about face, so that the banners and the guard were facing toward Rapallo, which lay by the sea two long downward curves of a road lined with people who would throw flowers and cry *Duce du-ce du-ce! Viva l'Italia fascista!*

They would doubletime, smartly, swiftly, elegantly, never blurring a note. The flags would stream in the wind. They would enter the town with tilted horns, tilted chins, under the banners strung from building to building.

MA È TEMPO DI CESSARE OGNI SCHERMAGLIA POLEMICA. GLI EVENTI INCALZANO. L'UNIONE DEGLI ITALIANI È ORMAI UN FATTO COMPIUTO. NESSUNO DEVE TURBARLA. NESSUNO LA TURBERÀ. È IL SEGNACOLO DELLA VITTORIA.

Two motorcycle couriers arrived first, minutes before the *Duce*. They braked, expressionless in their goggles, gave a gauntleted salute of the Caesars, shouted that the Duce di Fascismo was immediately behind them, and rode forward around the band, one to the right, one to the left.

The automobiles were suddenly there, while everybody was still watching the motorcyclists. The Duce was in his Alfa Romeo between two Mercedes. He was the first one out, doubletiming as soon as he was on the road. The bandmaster gave three salutes.

The Duce jogged in place, pulling down his tunic and setting his Sam Brown belt right. A gold sash looped his torso and hung from its hip knot down his left thigh. Il Aiutante danced beside him, his moustaches flapping, his chin high like the Duce's.

— *Avanti!* shouted the Duce.

— *Avanti a passo di corsa!* ordered the Aiutante.

— *Dietro front!* bellowed the bandmaster.

And down the road they went, *Giovanezza, Giovanezza!* thumping out in a wonder of shrill brass and resonant drum, the ancient gonfalon of Genoa jouncing beside the tricolor and the Fascist flag with its Italic ax bound in a bundle of sticks. A yellow dog and a brown joined them on the first curve, outpacing the guard and the color bearers.

The sad eyes of Max Beerbohm watched them as they bounced past his garden wall.

SONO OGGI FIERI E FEDELI GLI ITALIANI ALL' ESTERO!

The Mayor of Rapallo standing in a school of priests gave the salute of the Caesars as the band and the Duce trotted into the square in front of the City Hall. Children with bouquets of roses sang The Fascist Hymn. The Duce stood with his legs apart, his thumbs hooked in his belt, his chin high.

— *Camicie Nere!* he said. *Popolo di Rapallo!*

And made a speech. *Non vi è dubbio che giammai, come in questi ultimi tempi, l'Italia ebbe uno spirito militare così elevato.* And so forth.

Afterwards, the sun low over the bay of Tigullio, he visited the American poet Ezra Pound and admired his bust by Henri Gaudier-Brzeska.

— Why do you write poetry? he asked.
— To put my ideas in order, Ezra Pound said.
— Will you read us one of your poems?
Ezra Pound read two pages from his *Cantos*.
— *Ma quest'*, said Mussolini, *è divertente*!

AFTER NIGHTFALL, on my knees in the water, I dug. I scooped the sand out by handfuls. The deeper I went, the wetter the sand. This, *hercle*, was Rufus work.

The world is out there, independent of your will. I am here, behind the red furze of my beard, in my eyes, in my crazy knees and spine all but sprung. Demetrius the silversmith liked to say that he was a better silversmith than Lucius Domitius Ahenobarbus Nero Claudius Caesar Drusus Germanicus was an emperor. Old Nihil Magnus. I am a better slave than he is an emperor. You suck such consolation at your peril.

Give me, *frater*, fatter *consilia*. I remember the tombstone seen by some traveler in Asia Minor which a barbarian woman had set up, saying that she was the mother of two strapping sons, and that she had attended the grammar school in her old age to learn to read and write.

I remember the bitch the urchins found trapped in a wareroom, her ribs a corrugation down her pitiful body. She had eaten one of her puppies all except the head. She had eaten her shit. They brought me the bitch and pups, knowing me to be a fool, and when I gave her a bowl of mush she would not eat until her puppies had eaten. And when she ate she kept an eye on her brood. I renewed my devotions to Artemis. Rome has declined in virtue since Remus and Romulus pulled at the wolf's dugs. Would they had got her solicitude along with the milk.

I remember while licking my pan clean of its swill, dinners at which the vomitoria went around twice. You drink melted snow after you spew, chew a bit of ginger, and then go at the partridge breasts roasted in wine and garlic.

I remember tubs of leavings going off to the swine for which we would give thanks enough to run a sweet tickle into the ears of the gods. Once they brought a fat man here who wept like a woman while the smith soldered the shackles on his trotters. We watched the lard melt away day by day. He buckled fairly soon, pitching forward with his eyes rolled white and his tongue somewhere down his throat. His fellows beside him on the chain robbed him of his rags while he was still pitching in his agony. *Liber ille est,* someone said.

Voices, voices. I who had loved rhetoric like a mistress rarely hear two words together more articulate than the hinny of an ass. It was a voice hoarse as a raven over my shoulder when I was digging under my rock that said, *You're clearing a spring!*

Caepoculus, who had a chancre for his left eye. I knew him when he ran a little theater on the Via Scortilla where he was to be seen in a beaked mask, tail feathers on his butt, castanets on his fingers, dancing in the street to a music played by boy drummers and a fat whore with a tambourine who was so heavy that she had to be carried in a litter by slaves with gilded eyelids.

God, what an *ostentatio.* From that he came to this, no doubt by ways as mazy as Roman streets.

— Help me dig, and keep quiet, I said.

He hopped down beside me, hot as a stove with fever, and plunged his stringy arms into the sand. His one eye had horse terror in it, unblinking and staring. It was a bawdy eye in its day, eloquent of suggestion, when I had seen him cavorting in his feathers like an ostrich with piles, luring customers to his cellar where he presided as master of ceremonies over sottish musicians whose flesh was the color of lead. They played what they called antique Greek music while one of the boys humped a miserable old nanny goat, and the hippopotamine whore, she of the tamborine, danced the shimmy, and Caepoculus did the act for which he had a certain vogue. He lifted his tail feathers and farted in various styles announced beforehand in a solemn voice. A cultivated swain easing a squeak of sewer gas past the attention of a *hera.* A senator inadvertently punctuating his bombast with garlicky trumpetings. A poet's lyric toot while in rapture. A judge's authoritative *peditum.* A Christian's pious hiss. Imperator Nero's thunderous role and clap.

I remembered my geology, I remembered wells, the nature of earth, the evidence of the weeds, which were richer over my nook of the island than elsewhere. My hands bled, my nails tore. I had to stop Caepoculus and teach him how. I made a hole so deep my arms were in to the shoulders to get the next scoop of sand, wet sand, wet sand.

We damned the inlet with what we dug out, adding rocks for strength. The sea could not slosh in.

That is my shield against the Gorgon stare when the drums beat and the awful trumpets blow for the day's work in this monster of a ditch. I slog off to the latrines, to the messline, clanking in step with my brothers along the chain, to the great gully the sides of which are deep enough to make twilight of its bottom. For I am Rufus.

We found water.

I DO NOT KNOW where I am. I live in the oak Volscna, who is a thousand years old. Trees are people I have learned. There is too dark a difference between me and the animals. I cannot understand what they are doing, so busy all the time.

But trees like me, I think. I can hang from their boughs like a pear, an olive, an apple. They eat light. Volscna tells me tales, old, old tales. He remembers when elks were the kings of the world. He remembers the Etruscans, who watched the lightning with him. He has seen the sun black at noon. He calls me *one who moves in winter.*

I have been with ships on the sea, so far that the horizon is water all the way around, I have flown with the kestrels to their nests, I have been down to the bottom of the sea and watched spiders frail as hairs walking through forests of coral. The Consiliarii have abandoned me. I go by feel. I long to know the animals, to whom I am a stranger, perhaps forever.

In the oak Volscna I can lose myself in leaf after leaf, where light is fermented and all smells of a sharp green, in the mellow brown acorns, in the mistletoe. I can get close to the owls when they are asleep. At night we watch the stars, Volscna and I, the moon and the planets.

The Wooden Dove
of Archytas

INTO THE EYE of the wind it flew, lollop and bob as it butted rimples and funnels of air until it struck a balance and rode the void with a brave address. We all cried with delight.

My name is Aristopolites, called Trips. One of a wheen of tanlings enrolled in the gymnasium, where we learn to double the volume of a cube, chart harmonic proportions, wrestle, saltate, construe Homer, and sing, we also learn that the universe runs by strict laws which are at the mercy of chance.

The wooden dove was culver trim and very like, no gaudy anywhere about it. Its eyes were painted on, a circle with a dot inside, larger than natural, so that it goggled like an owl. It even had cronets made of byssus of the penna that splayed between its toes. It was the gazingstock of Taras for days before it flew. When important people came to see it, our handsomest oxboy would bring it on the flat of his hands, like Cora with the pomegranate, padding with his toes turned in. We littles, whose pizzles are no bigger than the gaster of a wasp, as the lizards tease us, were not allowed even to touch it.

When its works were explained to us at school, I told at table that Archytas the Pythagorean had made a wooden pigeon that could fly. Mama said I was neglecting my squash, Pappos crinkled his eyes, which is his way of laughing when his mouth is full, and Pappas asked how, by the cullions of Hermes.

— By steam, I said.

[38]

— By steam, Pappas said, to himself, the way you repeat something you want to remember.

— Out its bung, I suppose, he added, wiping honey from his beard and licking his fingers.

— Not only that, I said. The steam is going to be compressed inside, and will turn cogs with ratchets that will flap the wings. Most of the steam, it is true, will hiss out from under the tail and shoot the dove forward.

Pappos grinned with his eyes shut.

— I once saw a philosopher, he said, who had just left his house one morning, get wedged between two fat men who were walking deep in conversation, so that he was rolled right around to the opposite direction in the squeeze, and soon found himself at home again. *Short day!* he said to his good wife.

Pappas covered his face with his hands.

— Who was this? Mamma asked.

Krousithyros, our steward, fixed his distant look on his face, his whole thought on the elk of Thessaly.

— Order and chance, I said. But before I could explain myself Pappos was off again, and nothing takes priority over a grandfather except the drum of the militia in time of invasion.

— Then, he said, there was the philosopher who boiled his waterclock in the pot and timed it by the octopus he had bought for his dinner.

— Whatever! Mamma said.

Krousithyros whisked Pappos' eel pie away and gave him a compote of figs and curds, thinking even harder of elk.

— Pappas ka' Pappos, I said, will you come see the dove when it flies? It will go *whoosh*, and circle, they say, and then nobody knows what it will do. What if it flies out of sight, like a real dove?

SHE HAD COME UP to the house past the pigpen and the barn, past Scissor whisking out the buckboard for Uncle Billy, through the kitchen garden, and stood at the back steps, her moccasined feet together, her red hands crossed on her stomach. She wore a black derby with a jay's feather stuck in its band, a fringed shawl, a polka-dot dress over a blue gingham dress, the inmost skirts hanging lowest down her stout shins, which were wrapped in military leggings.

— How do, Breadcrust! Hanna said to her.

House niggers were on speaking terms with the Indians down to the creek, but that was all. Didn't they sit around the skillet in the middle of the floor, Tillman the dog and Okra the cat shoving in as members of the family in good standing, Anne and Jack and Tommy, all eating a stew maybe of squirrel poured piping hot over the hoecake, maybe of rabbit or even mush rat? And whatever it was, you could be sure it was as salty as brine. Or if it was hominy, they would have muscavados over the lot, and Dovey at it too, best she could.

— Hearn the hickwall, Anne Breadcrust said to Hanna, who was dashing slop over the hollyhocks.

— Hearn the ile.

— Do tell, Hanna said, putting her apron up over her mouth.

— Body die.

— Jesus take care of his own, Hanna said. I pay no tention to peckerwood. Huhu talk, she added.

Then she glanced over her shoulder into the kitchen, to see who might be listening, and leaned over the bannister. Anne Breadcrust stepped closer.

— *Mpatabiribiri wulisa kpang kpang*! Hanna said quickly, and showed her blue gums in a falsetto laugh.

Anne Breadcrust stood motionless, displeased.

— *Huh*! Hanna grunted, and went with dignity into the kitchen.

— Miss Fanny, Anne said, you reckon she come out?

She was speaking to whoever might hear her in the kitchen, where she saw the Medusa on the oven door, a churn, a safe with pitchers and bowls wrapped in cheesecloth. She put her feet together. She would wait.

— You say you hear an old owl? a voice came through the door.

— Hearn the peckerwood, too.

She would speak as they spoke, in their words. The voice was that of Aunt Amanda, a woman with more sense than Hanna and a witch to her people.

— Missy Manda, Anne Breadcrust called, I have a word for Miss Fanny, do you not mind.

She heard Hanna laughing, and a ringing of skillets. That comfortable, chucking sound was the meal sifter, and that slide and tap was the big knife cutting fatback for the whippoorwill peas, the hulls of which she could see in a dishpan on the porch.

And then there was Miss Fanny, six tortoise-shell combs in her hair. She had been transplanting cuttings, as it was time for the porch flowers to come inside, some to the root cellar, some to the dining room. She carried a cane geranium in one hand, a bent spoon in the other. Her hair was as black as a Cherokee's, she was fond of Dovey, and had often kindly asked how she did.

— Anne? she said, looking through the top of her gold-rimmed bifocals. Fall's coming on right fast, don't you think?

— A hard winter, Miss Fanny, she said quietly. See it in the stinkweed.

— Jack say so?

— See it in the squirrel tail.

Miss Fanny waited patiently for Anne to get around to what she had come to say. The silence was long.

— If you could let me have it, Anne said at last, I'd thank you for the matchbox.

— The matchbox! Miss Fanny said. What matchbox?

— The matchbox on the shelf in the kitchen.

— Whatever in the world *for?* Miss Fanny laughed, resetting her specs.

— Dovey dead.

She said it as if Miss Fanny ought to have known.

A ringdove, this Dovey, Miss Fanny knew, the kind that chimes before a shower and ruckles afterwards. Dovey had been presented to Miss Fanny on Jack Frost's finger, and it had cooed in her face. She had seen it looking out of the bib of Tommy's overalls with its button eyes. Silk Deer fed it from her hand with chickenfeed that she had given her.

— Did the dog get it? The cat?

— Tillman and Okra never bother Dovey, Miss Fanny.

She did not try to explain that Rattlesnake had been paid to take hunger for a dove from the dog and the cat. Those who were not the people could not understand.

— Wind blow the door to on Dovey, Miss Fanny. She die in my hands. Most pitiful sight you ever see.

— The door! Miss Fanny said.

— She was about to fly out, got out of Tommy's hand, flying up near the top and the door come to and catch her. Tommy cry and cry.

Miss Fanny raised her hands in sympathy.

— I hate it that it had to happen, she said.

Anne was shocked at the Presbyterian phrase but dismissed it as so much ignorance.

— The matchbox, she said, would make her a coffin. Such a pretty box. She would fit right in.

Hanna came out of the kitchen on the march, sifter in hand.

— Dove sat on Jesus' head the day He was baptize in the stream of Jordan, she said in her testifying voice. Norah sont a dove out from the Ark, and no place found hit for the sole of hits foot. Sont a nother, and hit brought back a live branch in hits bill. Scripture words, Scripture words, ever one I say. A bird sweet to Jesus is any dove. You must believe I'm truly sorry. Dovey with Jesus, Breadcrust.

— You welcome, Anne said. The ile sing all our death, in time.

WE GATHERED OUTSIDE our gymnasium where Archytas the Pythagorean was going to launch his dove from the courtyard. The steam it ran by was to come from copper kettles on a stove. Pappas came with me. Pappos showed up later, explaining that he might just see if the wrestlers and javelineers were in anything like shape for the summer games, but assured us that he did not expect to see any play-pretty of a wooden bird fly around whistling Sappho.

Two philosophers from Athenai had arrived in Taras a week before, still green from the crossing. One of them, Archytas told us, knew Aristophanes. The other remembered from childhood being shown a hale bald man with big feet and flat nose. Sokrates himself! We were all told from our first days in school that Archytas had letters from Plato in Sikilia, kept in their own jar.

Harp and flute signaled the arrival of the archons and the priests of Demeter and of Hermes Tree. Archytas almost didn't greet them, and paid them scant attention when a boy reminded him by tugging at his cloak. As it was, they had to accept a quick salute, ran through a prayer, and stood with the rest of us while the dove was brought out to the kettles.

Around us I heard charms against the eye of all lucklessness, the opinion that Archytas would scald himself and half the school, a hope that if the automatic bird did fly there would be rich travelers to Taras, Sicilian envy, Sidonian merchants who would ask us to supply them with wooden doves for their markets, the kindly regard of the gods.

On a grooved ramp pointing at a steep angle to the sky an oxboy set the dove and tested its wings by jiggling a mechanism that made it flap frantically, like a bird shooed from a roof.

Order and chance, I said to myself.

Archytas pointed now to this boy, now to that, and as his finger fell level Damos pulled a lever down and Karabion connected a tube to a kettle, Pantimos ran oil down a stick into the works of the dove, Babax fell to pumping the bellows. The archons and the priests began to step back, everybody stood on their toes, the better to see. The eyes of the dove stared, as if full of interest and hope, like a snake that has lifted its head to flick its tongue and listen in stillest silence.

MISS FANNY, TOO, went down to the creek beyond the bottom field where Anne Breadcrust and Jack Frost lived in a cabin that had been part of the slave compound, all that had survived. Only Indians would live in it now. The niggers had two-room cabins on the road, with newspapers on the walls, kerosene lamps, chickens, and a fig tree. Uncle Billy went as far as the edge of the field, explaining that he'd never been to the funeral of a game bird before, didn't expect the opportunity to arise again, and wanted some sense of what it was like.

Hanna and Miss Fanny went together, in Sunday hats. Hanna said she was going because there was something to everything an Indian did.

— There will be power, she said, and Scripture teaches that a dove is a bird close to the Lord.

She had a rabbit's foot on her person, a buckeye, and a horseshoe.

They found them sitting cross-legged with their backs to the cabin, Silk Deer and Tommy together, Anne and Jack Frost. Their red hands were on their knees. Before them, on a washtub turned upside down, lay Dovey in the matchbox, which was slid half open, so that one could see the silvery brown shoulder of a wing and the dull circle of a blind eye. Her beak was gaped, as if stilled in a last breath.

Miss Fanny nodded to each. Hanna stood behind, reticent.

— Dovey about to fly, Anne said to them. Her soul go up. It be happy where she go. It would be a good place to be.

A cane-bottomed chair had been placed for Miss Fanny, and beside it at a correct distance a keg for Hanna. Before each was a clean glass jar containing a feather.

Jack Frost began a kind of mumbled chant once they had taken their places. He kept time with a gourd rattler that he took from inside his Confederate greatcoat, causing Miss Fanny and Hanna to look at each other briefly, in recognition of their utter ignorance as to how Jack Frost came to be wearing part of Captain Mattison's parade uniform.

Anne joined the mumble, motionless as a statue except for her lips, and at some signal which they could not detect, Silk Deer and Tommy crept forward to the washtub and hunkered there, watching Dovey in her matchbox intently. Silk Deer cupped her thin long hands around her mouth.

— Tell her, Anne Breadcrust said, to find good medicine where she be. Tell her peck bitterweed and never mind this world no more. Take goldweed in her craw, for sunshine on her journey, sip springwater for the light of the moon.

— She bout to go, Jack Frost said, and shook his rattler the faster.

— Tell her, Anne said, snake been told, coon been told, jay been told.

— She going! Jack said with his eyes closed.

— Tell her, Anne said, Rabbit dance tonight. Tell her we dream.

Tommy looked up, Silk Deer looked up. The rattler ceased.

— We kick the door, Dovey! Anne cried. We kick the door!

— She gone, Jack Frost said.

ARCHYTAS FELL on his knees and looked at something under one of the kettles, signaling with a waving arm to Damos on the other side. There was a whomp and hiss in the air, and Pappas lifted me up so that I could see the dove leaking winter breaths of steam slide up the ramp, unfold its wings, and shoot upward. It whistled up like an arrow from a bow, fluttered with the stagger of a bat, and banking into a long high wheel, soared over the chronometer tower, the fane of Asklepios, the armory, the hills. We all cried with delight.

John Charles Tapner

A LANTERN held to his face showed which of the exiles in the
weave of the waves was the one who had insulted the Queen.
Their longboat had touched into the shingle and they jumped
from her prow, wet to the hips, to hand out women and boxes
and trunks with hummocked tops. They'd come across from Jersey
in a fog, calling on a tin trumpet that had the one flat ugly note
breaking into the music of the gannets and gulls, the bells of the
buoys, and the ruckus of windwash rolling the ocean at half dawn.

It was a grand thing to see them all remove their hats and bow
from the waist as the old one came from the boat. I had their
names on a list from the constable: Bachelet, Dessaignes, Fruchard,
Thomas, under proscription the lot, exiles living from pillar to
post.

Well over thirty years ago the first Napoleon died, in a rage they
say, on some island no bigger than this half the world around, and
the dust he raised will not settle in our time. But then the French
love a drum and adore a scarlet sash. Give them a snail to eat, a
tall bottle, a book with things ungodly and wild in it, and they will
follow a general with a moustache from shoulder to shoulder and
a brass band into heathendom and beyond, heel-deep in their own
gore.

He came across the brown sand, enlarged by the mist that had
bedeviled the island for days, a hank of vraic around one boot, he
never minding the hamp of it, his grizzard beard runched out from
the lappets of his redingote. The bonnet and frogged cape behind
him was his wife, fashed and tottering, flapping like a sea mew.

[46]

And yet another fluster of ruffles, wet and squealing gaily, was his daughter.

— *A very Beethoven of a wind!* he cried into my ear.

Holding the lantern aloft, I bade him welcome to the Bailiwick of Guernsey. I did not ask for papers. The peelers would remark upon that later.

His cunning eyes looked out of silken wrinkles, the eyes of a man easy with books and talk, restless and attentive, no rat's jinking from a hole more awake.

The daughter had a beauty which was, at that hour and mauger the blore, wearying toward length in the tooth and a sharpness of nose. She would later run away to the new world after a red sash of her own, but that's another story. From under her drenched cape she took two great oblong books. Shakespeare.

— Monsieur Martin, he said, pronouncing it French.

He took my hand in both of his and looked into the backrooms of my soul, my God what eyes! A knitch more on the fire and we stood in puddles before a blaze, swapping politenesses in a desperate sort of way, until *madame* said she would scream if she did not have a chair, a posset, and camphor on her temples.

—And what did I say? my goodwife Polly hissed as I fetched the rum.

— It is the way grandfolk act, I said. Consider the honor.

We put them up, we and the neighbors, for that hectic day, and that was that, for the nonce. They took the fine house in Hauteville Street, November 20, that belongs to Domaille, renting it for the year, even though the Alien Bill might shoot him out onto the sea again if all his grand talk had no effect on the high collars in London.

He had come here from Jersey, and he had come to Jersey from Belgium, where a number of exiles had fled, Doctor Raspail who wrote the home medical book, and the heretic Edgar Quinet. Louis Napoleon had scattered them all. Islanders study the newspaper carefuller than most.

We saw them every day or so moving about the rainy streets under umbrellas, and you could always, if you wanted, find the old one on a rock orating to the waves. He liked the young men who came from England and France to find him there, standing as if about to step higher, his cloak lifted out by the wind, saying things in Latin to the rack, to the silly puffins.

The man who made the daguerreotype of Tapner at the last came and took his likeness posed there on the rock.

Half the mail coming to and leaving the island was his. His little dog with a spot over his eye followed him everywhere. Senate was his name.

Two weeks after his arrival he turned up one morning and warmed his hands at our fire. Polly gave him the hint of a curtsy and pleaded that she had to go wring the neck of a hen.

Which reminded him, he said, of our curious taxes, each of us owing a chicken to the Queen by way of taxes. The *droit de poulet,* they call it in law.

— This paradise of fuchsias, he said. The green! Do you know, Citoyen Martin, that the greens get greener as one moves north up Europe? There is but one green, an acid, dull olive green, in the Mediterranean, but here on Guernsey there are forty greens, viridities of incredible brilliance, smaragdines, chartreuses, O leek and beryl and citrine. From tree to haw to lawn the eye passes more verdurous shades than in all Naples. You have a very Africa of green here, all the Brazils. And with the tenderest blue of the sky, the wild *forzando* of the fuchsia, and the glory of the jonquils to accent it. This is another Polynesia, with frost and fog.

And scarcely without taking a new breath he turned from the window and stared into my eyes.

— Tell me about Tapner, he said.

It was over Tapner that he had insulted the Queen. He had written a haughty letter to Palmerston himself that had been printed in the paper. I coughed and said nothing.

— It is, he went on, turning back to the window, a charming place indeed, your Saint-Pierre-Port. It is almost like a city for bustle when the paquebote is in, but in between, what serenity!

— It is not Paris, I said.

— Paris! he almost spat. Paris! he said with a long sigh. What is Paris but the avenue de l'Opéra? Snobs, merchants, politicians, boulevardiers, pedants, stupid women. If I fear *l'expioulcheune* it is because I would be in danger of having to return to all that *merde.* Can you show me the gibbet where Tapner died?

— Guernsey is an honest island, I said. We are all God-fearing people here, chapel for the most. We are nonconformists, like Milton, like Cromwell. We like to think of ourselves as independent and moral. There are about forty thousand souls on the islands, and there were but three in jail before the execution of Mr. Tapner. There are but two now, one of them a man kept there as a debtor by his wife, to whom he owes sixteen shillings. It is said that they love each other dearly, but as she likes to say, money is money. He has been there ten years.

His eyes got as big as pennies. I fancied he was about to take it all back about our lovely greens.

— I tell you this, I went on, to explain how little trouble we have among us. Tapner seemed to be the Devil his very self. His like is not common here, as I have no doubt it is in terrible places like London and Europe.

He smiled. He was, I'll vow, a gracious man.

— It's Mr. Barbet we'd have to see, I said. He's the jailor. He saw more of Tapner than I.

— You are the Queen's Provost, yes?

I nodded that I was, as he very well knew.

It was the opinion of Polly that this strange family was itself a signal contribution to the element of crime and impropriety on our island. The son François Victor had arrived and was said to be turning all the plays of Shakespeare into French, and as fast as he was doing them they were acting them in the evenings. We had the word here and the word there that duels with pokers had been sighted by passersby with a view of the windows, and that Agatha Tippy the seamstress had been asked to run up laughable clothes of purple and yellow stuff such as a mummer might wear.

Worse than that, the old one made up plays himself. We heard from their cook that one of them was about a lion that ate Christians in the time of the Romans. The old one took this part, wearing a false face that made him look like a cat the size of a pony, or a mustard owl. The story is out of an old book, as I explained to Polly. It is a tale in which an early Christian takes a thorn from the sore foot of a lion and, later, when it is his time to be a martyr and to fight wild beasts for the amusement of the Romans, it is this very lion to which he did the kindness that he faces, and instead of eating him the lion rolls over, returning the good deed.

— Grown people! said Polly. But then they're French. And there's another one has come, a *Miss* Drouet, if you please.

— A kinswoman? I'd asked.

— Foot, hooted Polly, nor frip of her was never a tenth cousin to any of that crew. What a nupson you can be, John Martin! The woman's a hoor. Your Frenchman, I've been told, has a wife for show and another woman for the sin of it, and they think no more of it than whistle up the drainpipe, hen tread the midden. What's more, they're all Papists, and not a moral among them anymore than a rat wears a flannel shimmy. She wasn't in her house a week before she sent for Hodge Perthmore to lay out a bed of flowers for her to make the letters of the alphabet vee and aitch. I tell you, it's like Mesopotamia in the Bible, kings and concubines. I hear the Vicar has had to put a vinegar rag to his temples for worrying about it.

In addition to which there was taking Shakespeare out of the table. That gave me more of a turn than their nesting habits.

— Yiss indeed, Tabitha Grimble told us, holding her saucer of tea at her chin and looking at us out of the side of her eyes. I have it on a word of honor. They take Shakespeare out of a table. The table cocks its leg, so to speak, and raps on the floor. I didn't sleep all night, thinking about it. And when it has rapped in a certain way, Shakespeare begins to write to them from the beyond, if you see what I mean.

Polly's eyes were out on stalks.

— They follow one scandal with the next!

— They have a board with an ABC on it, you understand, and a wee stand with three pegs it stands on, and they touch this ever so lightly with their fingertips, and this thingumabob moves about and spells words, do you see?

— But of course they're pushing it where they want it to go, I protested.

— On no! said Tabitha. Their eyes are shut tight. It's her, the daughter, copies down what Shakespeare . . .

— Old Scratch, Polly corrected.

— *Who* are they? Tabitha said. I know they're prominent people, and gentry as they have it in France, and that they're in bad with their king over there. So oriental, the French, wouldn't you say?

— They all have the same Christian names, Polly said, locating another scandal. The mother is Adèle, the daughter is Adèle; father and son are both Victor. But what's that when they haven't no more gumption than my hens and break the seventh commandment and eat snails.

— And was taken off Jersey by the Law and brought here, Tabitha said, because of something disrespectful of the Queen he put in a newspaper. I wonder that they don't bundle the lot of them back to France.

— What, John, did he say in the newspaper? Was it that letter about Tapner?

— He tried to keep Tapner from being hanged, I explained. He has spoken against capital punishment for years. On the lines, as I understand it, that two wrongs don't make a right. Says its makes a murderer of society.

Tabitha looked outrage from her eyes. Polly patted her foot.

— I wonder how he would have talked, I said, if he had known Tapner?

HE WORE HIS GREATCOAT, for the day was raw. We met, as agreed, before the prison, up the hill from the government buildings. I had told him how he could identify the plain granite building by the G cut in the arch of its gate, and over the G a crown. He was there when I arrived, a cunning look of amusement in his eyes.

— The G, he said, pointing up, and the crown.

I shook hands with him in the French manner, and pulled the bell that brought a warder to let us in. The jailor was on the lookout for us, and came forward bearing a ring of keys.

— Barbet, I said, this is Vicomte Hugo, the distinguished French writer who's taking refuge on our shores because he doesn't recognize Napoleon the Third as Emperor of his country. Vicomte, High Sheriff Barbet.

— Never *Vicomte*, he said, shaking a playful finger at me. *Mister* is all a man needs, or if you prefer, *Citizen Hugo*, unless, of course, one is a *High Sheriff*.

His bow to Barbet from the waist embarrassed us both. Barbet winked, as if to say that we had a slippery one on our hands.

— I want, Monsieur Hugo said, quite simply to see the cell of John Charles Tapner. And, if it is permitted, where he died.

He pronounced him Zhon Sharl Topnair.

— Well, Barbet said, you are welcome to Barbet House, as those adept at hamesucn and sneakbudging call my establishment.

I realized that Monsieur Hugo understood very little English. He and I spoke French, if you can call my schoolboy's French French. When Barbet spoke, Hugo had that look in his eye which was part bluff and part hope that what was being said did not require comment or answer.

We passed through Barbet's apartments and could see his wife and daughter peeling carrots and potatoes.

Tapner's cell, when we reached it down a cold white corridor, had a black door. Long iron hinges traversed its width.

— It is occupied, you understand, Barbet explained as he found the key and unlocked the narrow black door with such a feeling of blankness about it, as if it had no right to any feature or ornament.

Inside there was a woman, shivering. Her dress was thin, her shoes worn out, and her only other garment, a kind of party coat, once pink, had been some grand lady's wrap for summer wear. She sat huddled on a cot before a small brick fireplace that had nothing in it.

— She is a thief, Barbet said as if she were not there, an Irish thief.

Hugo looked at her with pity, but said nothing. I think he wanted to speak, but restrained himself. Instead, he looked carefully at the ferociously plain walls, at the little window with its two black bars.

— She has been arraigned? he asked in a soft, conversational tone.

— And is waiting for her sentence, Barbet said.

— What will it likely be?

— Australia, I suppose. These cells are way stations, you might call them. The prisoners go from here to another prison, to deportation, or to the gallows. Across the way you can see the Mill Bank block, where the prisoners are serving out time. There they may not speak, or sing, or whistle.

— Why, said Hugo, does that woman not have a fire to sit by?

— No fires ever, Barbet said, however cold it gets, except by doctor's orders.

Barbet opened the cell next to Tapner's. It was empty, and somehow looked less desolate than the other because it was empty. Some prisoner had decorated the whitewashed wall. He had written the words *war, history,* and *Cain.* And around these unarticulated words he had drawn a veritable navy of all sorts of ships, accurately but without any grace of line.

Monsieur Hugo stood on the bed and peered out the high window.

— One can see Sark, he said. And ships on the horizon. That woman back there, he said in the same tone of voice, is phthisical. I should also think that she is dying.

Barbet glanced at me. This Monsieur Hugo was already overstepping himself.

— She is not bright, Barbet offered. For days she has been asking if her grandmother is still alive. Not that she will tell us who her grandmother is, mind you. Just that, the everlasting question if her grandmother's alive.

We were shown a cell for particular punishment, where the window was too high to see out of, and where the bed was a mere bench.

— Well, look here! Barbet said. Here's more whitewash ruined.

A whole wall was drawn over with a maze. It was a Troy Town or garden path that doubles and doubles on itself, but far more confused.

Monsieur Hugo followed some of it with his finger, and laughed.

— I suppose these buggers have no reason to feel that they should be considerate of my walls, Barbet said.

— No! Monsieur Hugo said, brightening his face into a glorious grin. But no, never, none whatsoever!

I had never seen him so merry. Barbet laughed too, God knows why. Hugo clapped him on the shoulder, laughing the harder. Then he put his hands deep in his pockets and his beard on his chest, a characteristic way of walking along for him. I've noticed it often. Suddenly he looked up at me with utter mischief on his face, like Mr. Punch.

Of the seven cells in this wing of the prison one is fitted out as a chapel. It has a wooden chair in a corner for the minister and several rows of backless benches for the worshipers, with hymnals and tracts arranged upon them neatly.

With the largest of his keys Barbet opened a stoutly barred door and let us into an oblong court as bare of any object as an empty box. On three sides, high walls. The fourth side was the other half of the prison. Its narrow windows had panes, with white bars behind the glass.

It had begun to rain. We could see the branches of a tree in the sheriff's garden beyond the wall, fog caught in them like lambs-wool. Barbet coughed and rocked on his heels, making his coat swing like a bell.

The jailor Pearce, whose sister is one of Polly's cronies, came into the court, bringing with him a young man of good build.

— On his way, Barbet said, to ten years in Botany Bay, for theft.

He wore canvas trousers, a wool jacket, and a cap with a long bill. Pearce gave us good morning. Voices in that empty court sounded as hollow as across a field. The young man did not look at us.

Barbet took us to a kind of shed, without windows, that had been built onto the back of the prison. In here was the gallows.

— There are, as you may count, thirteen steps up. The con-demned stands there, on that trap, and drops through when that bar is slid away. I think we might do it with more courage if the executions were still in the old way, in front of the prison, with a crowd to watch and cheer, and with the charges read in a strong voice before the drop.

— Tapner now, as you've come to hear about him, was won-drous calm, careless you might say, in his last days. Look here.

Barbet took a daguerreotype from his pocket.

— This was made just before he was hanged. We had the man with his apparatus into the cell. There was, as you can see, a good light. Look at that broad grin.

It was, indeed, the picture of a man pleased with himself.

— I fair had to shout at him, *don't smile! You must look seri-ous in your picture. You are about to stand in judgment before your Maker.* You would think it was a thing impossible, but he kept to his smile. He said it was well known that one should always smile when having one's likeness taken.

— He was a kind of gentleman, you know. He worked at a government post until gin and pilfering got the better of his character.

— He was young, Monsieur Hugo said.

— He lived with two women, sisters, married to one, the lover of the other. He was of a Woolwich family, honest people they said at the trial. His father was a religious man. When the wife came for a last visit, she was heartbroken. She knew all about his carryings on with her sister. She forgave him all. The murder too, I suppose. These people are shocking.

— Before he was hanged, Tapner was presented with a prayer book by the minister. *Read that if you are guilty*, the minister said. *I am not guilty*, Tapner said. *Read those prayers anyway. We are all sinners.* An hour later the minister found Tapner reading the book, water standing in his eyes.

— Tapner had insured his life for five-hundred pound, the premiums for which took his whole income. He ran his household with what he could steal.

— And did the insurance company pay up? Monsieur Hugo asked.

— Of course not.

— Not even the premiums?

— Oh no! It would have been a scandal to do that.

— See how virtuously an insurance company can rob a widow, Monsieur Hugo said. It seems the genius of this century is that it can find a good reason for anything. Did Tapner know about my letter to Palmerston?

— Oh yes, Barbet said. And he was very grateful. He felt that it was a large thing for you to do. He knew that it was useless, of course. Justice is justice.

— The tenth of February he was hanged. He was thirty-one. In all our years of hangings we had always paraded the condemned through the streets, by the school, down the High Street, and through the market. Six soldiers went before, rolling drums in a slow march, and the Queen's man brought the mace behind. We had not had a hanging for a full twenty-five years. Times change, as they say. It did not seem modern to walk him around the town, the rope already fitted to his neck. So Tapner was hanged privately here, in this dark place. *For I am the resurrection and the life* were the last words he heard. He himself had nothing at all to say. His shirt was wet with a cold sweat when we tied on the hood, and his eyes were those of a suffering animal.

Monsieur Hugo placed a foot on the bottom step up to the gallows and looked at the crossbeam where the rope would have been secured. We could hear rain on the roof.

— Once Tapner dropped through the trap, Barbet said, the Queen's man, the chaplain, and the judge all left quickly. We waited an hour before we cut him down. After keeping back a bit of the rope for a remembrance, I put it on the fire. It is a thing that has always been done.

FROM THE GIBBET we three walked down Market Street to that maze of brick courts and dark passageways nigh the cattlepens behind which we came to Potter's Field, as forsaken and cheerless a place as you will find on the island. A stubborn bramble choked the corners of its low wall, and its meadow grass, matted now and dank with rain, needed a thorough coursing of sickle and rake.

— Over there, Barbet nodded toward a red roof showing above an orchard, is the Frenchman Béasse's house. Come and look over the wall. Like as not we'll see Tommy Didder.

— And who is he? Monsieur Hugo said from the lappets of his greatcoat.

— His gardner, as was. And his hangman.

— Béasse, I explained, goes back twenty year or so, an officer in the campaigns in the Peninsula.

— With my father, Monsieur Hugo said. You say that he was hanged? Here?

— Well, Barbet said, he killed his own child, a bastard he had by his cook, and tried to hide the little body over there in that orchard. The state of the cook had been noticed, and its change, and with no tyke in evidence, our suspicions were aroused. The gardner Didder found it himself. They'd run a stick right through it, from mouth to fundament, a sight so pitiful the crowner shouted at the jury that their duty was to get Béasse into an eternity of hell fire as fast as they could return a verdict of Guilty.

He was taken through the streets, and the soldiers made way for people to spit on him.

— The times have changed, I said. The feeling was never so fierce among the people when Miss Saujon's body was found with her throat cut from ear to ear, and all the evidence showed that Tapner had doubtless done it.

— Doubtless?

— O, no doubt, Mister Hugo, Barbet said. They were seeing each other in a sinful way. Moral degeneracy in one respect leads to any other. Tapner had the Devil in him. God knows what caused him to cut the poor woman's throat. But cut it he did. They found his shirt as bloody as a butcher's.

We'd reached the wall, and looked over. The garden was all mulched and under beds of hay. Didder was nowhere in sight.

— He has his memories, Barbet said. He had to accuse, and to hang the man he was gardner to. If ever a man felt the sharpness of a judgment, it was Béasse. The bailly, you see, was his best friend. They were like brothers here on the island. His ears took the sentence of hanging from the mouth of the man he loved most. Their eyes never once met in the courtroom. And Didder, his gardner, hanged him. I can show you his trap, as well as Tapner's. We make a new one every time. I have them in a shed at the jail.

— No, Monsieur Hugo said, but I'll see Tapner's grave, if you'll show it to me.

Stones no bigger than bricks marked the plots in that dreary, wet ground, and they were smothered in grass all a gnarl. We got the sexton, who had been opening a grave for a pauper, to help us with the finding.

— He was buried in his own clothes, Barbet said, which by our law are his. In London, you know, all the effects of the condemned belong to the hangman. But he has to provide a shroud. You wouldn't put even the damned indecent into their graves.

The day was thickening with fog. Tapner's stone was shiny with mist when we found it. The sexton pushed down the grass with his boot so that we could read the begrudging JCT 1854 cut on it with a degree of neatness.

— Did you bury Tapner? Monsieur Hugo asked the sexton.

— Beg pardon, Sir?

The brogue had raddled him. I put the question myself.

— This booger here? Yiss. Him what was a fornicator and never did a stroke of work in his life. Sat on a stool in a room with a stove. Two given to falling in fits, the stable lad and a girl from the Eldridge farm, came to touch the corpse. If it's took off their affliction nobody has thought to tell me.

Monsieur stooped and broke off a blade of grass from Tapner's grave and put it in the pages of a tablet he had in his pocket. Barbet looked at him as if he were a prize fool if ever one set foot on Guernsey.

— Are you satisfied, then, Mister Hugo? he asked. This damp is getting into my bones and my feet are starting to perish.

A silence. I had my thoughts, confused as they were, but I would remember that moment later, when there was a sort of fellowship among us there at Tapner's grave, little as any of us understood anything of each other. I remembered it when he wrote yet more letters, this time to America, to demand of those stout and troubled people that they not hang the man John Brown. I remembered it when his daughter followed the English soldier to Newfoundland and sent back the lie that she was his wife.

— And now, Mister Hugo, Barbet said as a pleasantry that did not sound like one, are you quite satisfied?

— I am told, he said, that your minister Monsieur Palmerston wears all the time white gloves.

He held his hands, as freckled and wrinkled as his face, out in the raw air, for us to see.

— I do not.

Au Tombeau de Charles Fourier

I

Here, chittering down the boulevard Raspail in her automobile, is Miss Gertrude Stein of Alleghany, Pennsylvania, a town she has no memory of at all and which no longer exists, and of Oakland, California, where as she will tell you, there is no there there.

She has delivered babies in Baltimore tenements, dissected cadavers at The Johns Hopkins Medical School, and studied philosophy and psychology under William James at Harvard. She has cut her hair short to look like a Roman emperor and to be modern.

She has cut her hair short because behind her back Hemingway talked about her immigrant coiffure and steerage clothes and because Picasso had painted her portrait with her elbows on her knees in allusion to Degas' Mary Cassatt sitting that way.

And what was there to do after that but to cut one's hair, to end that chrysalis time. So many beginnings all her life made Gertrude Stein Gertrude Stein. She walked from the Luxembourg Gardens to the butte Montmarte to sit for Picasso and to be modern.

She has flown in an airplane since then and with her foot on the gas like Wilbur Wright flying at Le Mans and her Printemps scarf fluttering behind her like Blériot's crossing the Sleeve, the Friedmann, the Clichy, the Raspail were hers, all hers.

She is driving home from reading The Katzenjammer Kids to Pablo. And The Toonerville Trolley and Krazy Kat. Genius is as wide as from here to yonder. Long ago, William James said in a lecture, the earth was thought to be an animal as yes it is.

Its skin is water, air, and rock. It is the horse, the wheel, and the wagon all in one. A single intelligence permeates its every part, from the waves of the ocean of light to the still hardnesss of coal and diamond deep down in the inmost dark.

In Professor James the nineteenth century had its great whoopee, saw all as the lyric prospect of a curve which we were about to take at full speed, but mistaking the wild synclitic headlong for propinquity to an ideal, we let the fire die in the engine.

And after dinner the Vanderbilts had the servants bring in baskets of Nymphenburg china which they smashed against the wall, cup by beautiful cup, for the fun of it. We let the fire die in the engine. Marguerites the meanwhile bloomed at Les Eyzies de Tayac.

La série distribue les harmonies : les attractions sont proportionelles aux destinées.

II

And Elizabeth Gourley Flynn in shirtsleeves marched with the striking silk workers in Paterson. Between quiet and glory the usurers gobbling with three chins were spreading their *immondices* of bank money which is not money, no it is not money.

It is not the sou in the concierge's fist nor the honest buck in the farmer's. Between Picasso's mandolin and pipe and *Le Figaro* bright on a tabletop they forced their muck of credit and interest, the business of business, not of things.

What could Rockefeller or Morgan care that the only time in history the command *Beh*-TELLion! *Lee ye doon!* was given was to the 96th Picton's Gordon Highlanders at Quatre Bras when Wellington drove a charge of cavalry over their heads.

Alice in her ribbons! Alice in a kilt! *C'était magnifique et c'était la guerre.* And down went the bagpipes missing never a skirl, and down went the black banners touching never a blade of Belgian grass and red coats and sabres flew over their heads.

The horses streamed over their heads even though they were advancing with bayonets *en frise.* Lord, what porridgy comments must have sizzled all burr and crack on what by fook the daff and thringing Sassenach duke thought the hoor's piss he was doing.

Here she honked her klaxon at a moustached and top-hatted old type crossing the Raspail like a snail on glue, who cried out *Espèce de pignouf! Depuis la Révolution les rues sont au peuple!* Whereupon she honked back at him *Shave and a haircut, two bits.*

And Wellington's cavalry flowed like so many Nijinskys over Wellington's Highland Infantry and that was the glory that was fading from the world and all for money that is not money and Alice was waiting for her at home on the rue de Fleurus, next left.

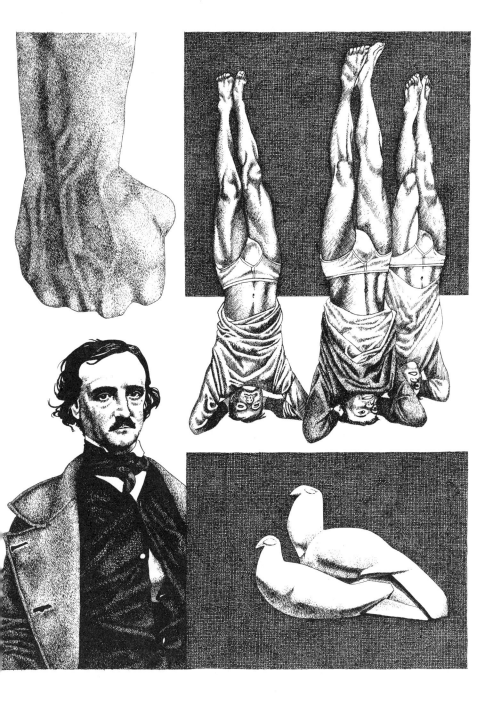

Wasps fly backwards in figure eights from their paper nests memorizing with complex eye and simple brain the map of colors and fragrances by which they can know their way home again, in lefthand light that bounces through righthand light, crisscross.

The queen when she has chosen a site for a nest flies in wider eights than the cursory and efficiently warped ovals of scouts out to forage or the wiggly eights of trepidous adolescents on their timid first flight out from their hexagons shy but singing.

III

Ogo in his stringbean bonnet dances under the Sahara moon. That is not a sugarcane whistle we think he is playing. It's his squeaky little voice so high, so high. He alone of all the creatures God made has no twin, none to trot by, none to nuzzle.

None that he can mount, now that time's begun. The mud houses of Ogol in the rocky scrub country of the great Niger bend crowd their brown cubes under tall baobabs and cool acacias. Walls facing the trembling light of the Sahara are the color of pale biscuit.

The shadowed walls are the strong bister of red cattle. The square towers of the granaries rise higher than the houses. Ogotemmêli, the Dogon metaphysician, sits in his chicken yard, blind, telling of Ogo and Amma, his hands clasped behind his head.

He wears the oblong tabard of brown burlap which old men might wear in the freedom of the house. His grizzled beard is trimmed neat and close. He is teaching the clever *frangi* the history of the world, by command of the Hogon of Ogol.

He teaches him the structure and meaning of the world. The man Griaule, the *frangi*, who comes every year in his *aliplani*, sits before him. He makes marks along thin blue lines on pressed white pulpwood fiber finer than linen, putting a mark for every word.

Ogotemmêli touches the silver stylus with which Griaule makes the marks, runs his fingers over the thin leaves where the marks are put. The Hogon had decided: tell the white man who for fifteen years has come to Ogol asking, asking, tell him everything.

He already knows many things, the rites, the sacrifices, the order of the families, the great days. But never yet have they told him the inmost things, for fear that he would not understand. It was Ogotemmêli at the council who thought that he might understand.

He is like a ten-year-old child, but he is uncommonly bright, he had said to the Hogon. Might he not understand the system and the harmonies if they were explained to him slowly and carefully, as one instructs a boy? Besides, he gives our words to others.

The Hogon spoke with the Hogon of their brother people in the valley, who spoke with Hogons over near the sea, up and down the river, until it was decided that the white man was to know. So Ogotemmêli lights his pipe. Good thoughts come from tobacco.

IV

In the beginning, he said, there existed God and nothing. God, Amma, was rolled up in himself like an egg. He was *amma talu gunnu*, a tight knot of being. Nothing else was. Only Amma. He was a collarbone made of four collarbones and he was round.

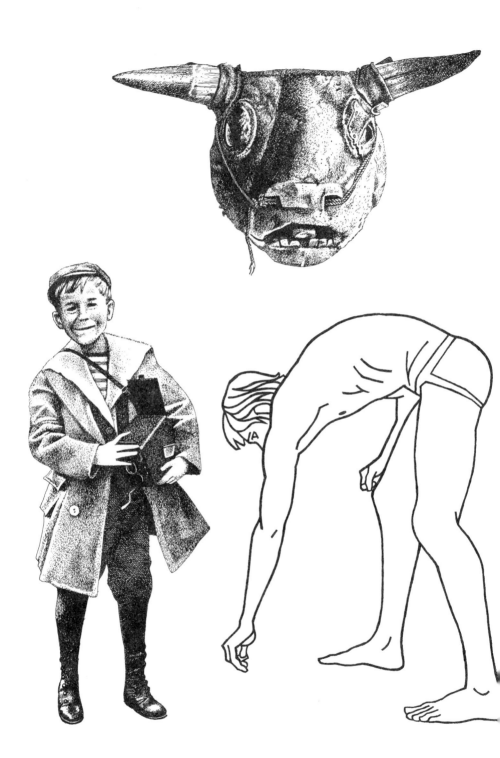

You have heard the Dogon say: the four collarbones of Amma are rolled up together like a ball. Amma is the Hogon of order, the great spendthrift of being. He squanders all, generosity unlimited, and arranges what he squanders into an order, the world.

Amma plus one is fourteen. Say *Amma* and you have said *space*. For Amma to squander he needed space. He is space itself and only needed to move himself outward, to swell himself out, like light from the sun, like wind from the mountains, like thunder.

Three days after Picasso learned the word *moose* he was pronouncing it *muse*. It has a nose the likes of which you see on critics but the horns they have still *verdaduramente* the glory of God in them from the week of creation, a beast part hill, part tree.

You love all that's primeval, Gertrude says, while I love all that's newer than tomorrow. What is cubism but tilting our vision, ceasing to pretend that we see with our heads in a clamp? Each eye sees, that is Cézanne's lesson, eyes move in looking, that is yours.

Matisse began to include the edges especially of women as they are seen a little more to the left than you would see if the right is there and a little more to the right than you would see if the left is here, a primitive and intelligent way of looking.

And then with Spanish generosity Pablo gives us more tilt of head everywhere, even in the middle of things, like Mercator's map. She has told him with an earnestness that makes him whinny that if he were to fly he would see that the world is a cubist painting.

In an aeroplane? Braque and I wanted to build one, can you imagine? But only for a little while. We liked the shape, the circles of the wheels so balanced with the lines of the body. But no, Jertrude old girl, you'll never get me up in one of those things.

An *alcool framboise* at the Closerie: the laughter of Apollinaire and Picasso, tears running down their cheeks, and Gertrude's cackle right along with them, pounding each other's backs, was there anything like it? One sees a lot of gypsies, the waiter said.

V

Of Diktynna not even the waff of a talus as she slips behind a sycamore, nor the rax of her talbots as they up and pad sprag after the crash of her toggery. Her cats, though, his cats are here, tabby and pied, get of the friends of the enemy of silver.

He lies under a slant stone bearing at its corners parabola, hyperbola, circle, ellipse. Bones, buttons, dust of flesh. High the jugal line would jut, and mortal holes gape where once there had been the iambus of his wink, a dust of flowers sifted through his ribs.

The fluid tongue is now trash. The bones of his thin fingers lie crossed over the immortally integral crocket of pubic hair, inert with silicon, gray and zinziber, mingled now with the rubble and pollen of his landlady's hydrangeas and Charles Gide's last roses.

La série distribue les harmonies, the stone reads. *Les attractions sont proportionelles aux destinées.* Elm leaves lie crisp and stricken upon the lettering. A porcelain wreath of some antiquity shares the moss and lichen that are claiming the slab.

ICI SONT DEPOSES LES RESTES
DE
CHARLES FOURIER
NE A BESANCON LE 7 AVRIL 1772
MORT A PARIS LE 10 OCTOBRE 1837

The series distributes the harmonies. Linnaeus died when he was six, Buffon when he was sixteen, Cuvier was his contemporary. Swedenborg died the week before he was born. All searched out the harmonies, the affinities, the kinship of the orders of nature.

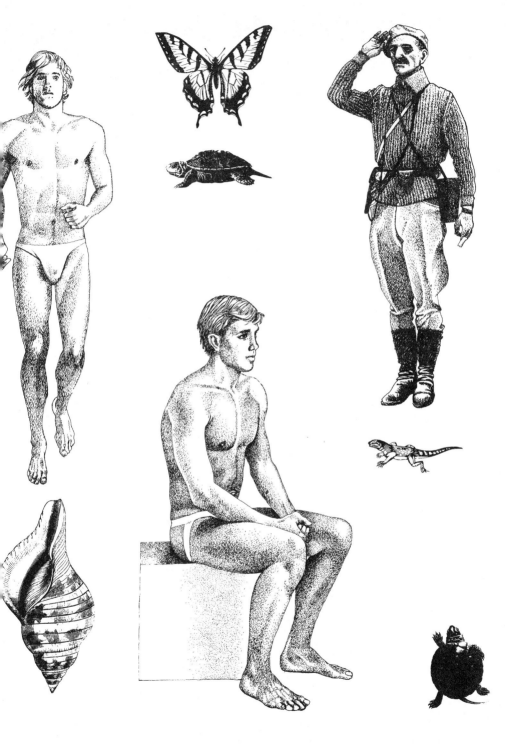

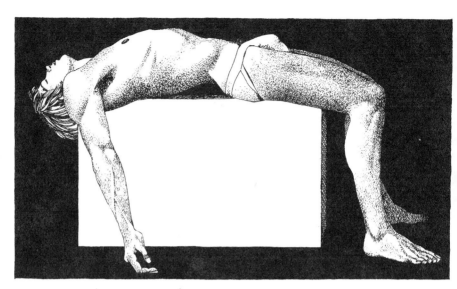

All of nature is series and pivot, like Pythagoras' numbers, like the transmutations of light. Give me a sparrow, he said, a leaf, a fish, a wasp, an ox, and I will show you the harmony of its place in its chord, the phrase, the movement, the concerto, the all.

The morning before we went to Fourier's grave we watched President Giscard-d'Estaing walk from his inaugural up the Champs Elysées to the Arc, republican, pedestrian, affable. There was no *La Marseillaise,* no parade. Hatless he strode along alone.

But if it had been the month of Floréal in the Year 120, first pentatone of the Harmony, the sillima trees a water of *hsiao chung* and chinkled pyrite, we might have seen a scout of the Hordes and two little girls in Romany finery dancing with a ginger bear.

VI

The air rich with the peculiarly Parisian aroma of roasting chestnuts, quagga droppings, and baskets of marigolds, two little girls in Romany finery shimmy down the Elysées behind their elder brother tapping a timbrel above his head as he strides.

He twirls it high and brings it down with a clash and a *hoodah!* against the naked brown of his thigh. An elder recommends to his gaffers over their wine that they eye the nisser and the kobold, outriders as they read the emblems of the Chrysanthemum Horde.

They and the Goldenrods are of the Phalanstery Nora Joyce, them skirts as dazzled in the tuck and ruff as a margery prater all the colors of pepper from Floréal to Vendémiaire, Paraguay green, English blue, and a red to grace the boot of a Manchu khan.

Chilimindra and Gazella the girls, Crispin the brother, Strummel Jark the bear. Police of the Gardens and Corporals of Fine Tone salute as they pass, children all, clad by tribe, or naked except for the boondoggle of their clan and their doggy dignity.

Farther back, coming through the Arc, bouncing to drums, a zebra patrol enters the Elysées with a fanfare of E-flat trumpets. The colors out front are those of the XXI Hungarian Typhoons, Company Marie Laurencin, Magyar reds and pinks.

The guidons jig from under the arch, Phalanx Petulengro, Apollinaire, Souza Andrade, Marcel Griaule, Max de Bégouën. Chilimindra, Gazella, and Crispin, ten, eleven, and twelve, are champion makers of fudge, masters of zebras, of cobbling and of knots.

They are masters of horns and flowers, of printing and dancing, of the cello and cartography, of crystals and snakes, of polyhedral tensegrities and cetacean speech, of history and embroidery. They are companions palatine of the Great Bear of the Dnieper.

The circle on Fourier's tomb means friendship, the hyperbola ambition, the ellipse love, the parabola family. The Little Hordes are two thirds boys and one third tomboys, the Little Bands are two thirds girls and one third shy mama's boys.

Their mounts are zebras for the Hordes and quaggas for the Bands. The Grand Hordes, of Vestals in rawhide, prancing to trumpets, of naked Spartans with javelins and winebowl hairdos, of the Pioneers Major and Minor, are mounted all on tarpans.

VII

It was in Huffman's Meadow out from Dayton on the way to Xenia that we mastered flying around a honey locust and Mr. Root the editor of *Gleanings in Bee Culture* saw us. We came through the film first in wild winds over the sands at Kill Devil Hill.

We came over the sands at Kitty Hawk, our huffer and zinger made of iron with feet that kicked in its heart where lightning burst the blood of blue grandfather scum rotted and gunked from the time of the chicken lizards. Our wings were made of cloth.

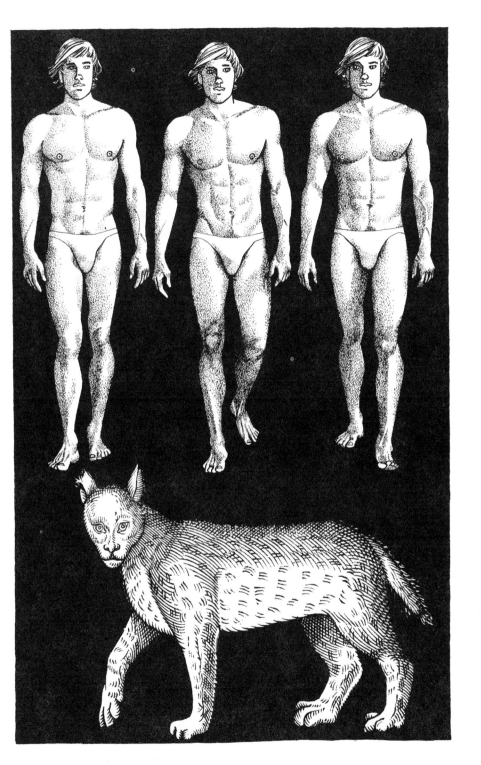

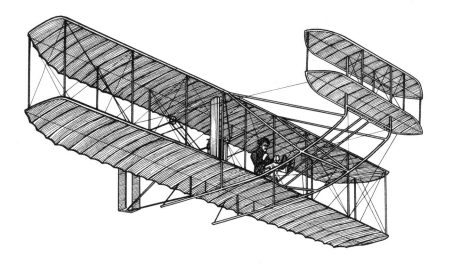

Our wings were made of splinters and knitten flax, our eyes were another's and nothing was wholly right for shape or go. We could rock in rising and settling like a hornet, ride like a bee, but the figure eight of the wasp, or a clapfling proper, we could not do.

You cannot forage until you can twist your loop, shimmer of red on the up, shake of green on the down, with wood to chew on every bought, and a pear gone wine beyond the briars, and a liquor of roses sweet as wives drenching all, wind and light combing light.

Ogotemmêli lifted his head, cupping his hand behind his ear. There was something interesting in the air. *Dougodyé*, he said. *I hear the step of Dougodyé.* A young shepherd approached in sunglasses, a French undershirt, and wide baggy Dogon trousers.

Innekouzou's cow, he said with a grin, *has thrown twin calves. Give me a sou. Amma numo*, said Ogotemmêli, *vira aduno vo vaniemu! Come, Brother Griollu, lead me to the baobab, where we can drink beer for the blessed ancestors. Twin calves, I'll be bound!*

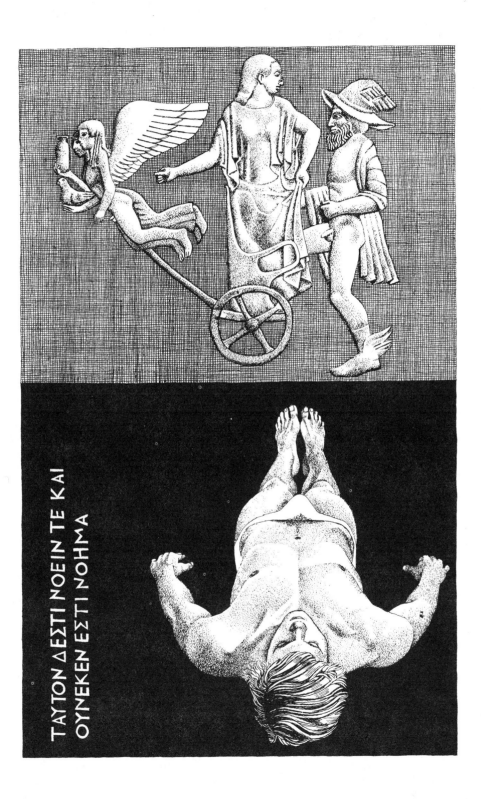

ΤΑΥΤΟΝ Δ ΕΣΤΙ ΝΟΕΙΝ ΤΕ ΚΑΙ
ΟΥΝΕΚΕΝ ΕΣΤΙ ΝΟΗΜΑ

We must go honor the sign of twins, a blessing that refreshes me to hear. He went into his house with blind caution and came back in his Phrygian cap, his checkerboard tabard of goat's wool, and a sou for Dougodyé. The armpit drums and Ogo fife had begun.

They walked between granaries and houses, by altars, to the great baobab. *Everything that reaches up to God must be firmly rooted,* Ogotemmêli said, bowing to the bows which he knew were being made to his rank, his blind steps sure. Twin calves!

A woman with many beads of cowries and beaten gold *nummo* put a gourd of cool beer into his long fingers. Elders with staves came gravely to the tree, talking of other twins in other days, holding cups to the calabash. *This too,* said Ogotemmêli, *is worship.*

VIII

Quagga, brother of the Herero and Himba, ran in gray herds silver through the mimosa. The mares pranced out before, smelling for lioness, foals and yearlings swirled girlishly behind, and the stallions, maned and haughty, confidently trotted at the rear.

Orangutans furiously pulled grass and put it on their heads as the quaggas streamed by. *O moon*, cried the orangutans, *O moon*. Elephants rolled their trunks, by which they meant that you never go to the waterhole except to find there a family of nickering quaggas.

They come to the water as picky as antelopes, their honest eyes looking at everything, their nostrils atick with the dusty smell of elephant, green fragrance of water, blunt odor of rhinoceros, the far stink of panther and the carrion cough of hyena.

Stepping to trumpet and snare they were to have been the mounts for patrols foraging for virtue from phalanx to phalanx, galloping out under banners citron and blue, captained by ten-year-olds, Bears of Artemis braceleted with silver snakes.

She rides, this Jeanne or Louise, with the poise of an Iroquois and the hauteur of a Cherokee. She wears, *transactu tempore*, like her flowery troop, *braccae phrygiae*, persimmon trousers open on a dapper bias from hip to inner thigh, tucked into canvas boots.

She wears, like the boys, a buttonless vest embroidered with frets and florets, a neckerchief as yellow as the Icelandic buttercup, and a tam sporting the gray and white ribbons of the Phalanx Jules Laforgue, Escadrille Orage XI, Grammarian First Class.

They are off, quaggas, girls, boys, and a shuffle of forty raccoons kept in pod by Weimaraner corporals. Of going a progress the raccoons understand nothing, but Weimaraners trained to shepherd raccoons on marches between phalanxes they understand.

The Weimaraners understand the Little Hordes, Quagga masters and spadgers after Harmonian honor, gosling cadets in the affinities, the *gammes*, who are out to gather optima, centibonum by centibonum, pips and stars and blue ribbons and duck feathers.

For getting the raccoons from phalanx to phalanx hale and chipper, five centibona. For taking over the chores of the local goslings, fifteen. For general good nature, judged by the Police of Tone and Manners, twenty. For coining a new word, twenty-five.

Ο ΔΕ ΧΡΟΝΟΣ ΕΝ ΧΡΟΝΩ ΟΥ ΓΙΝΕΤΑΙ

IX

For spending the day with an elder and looking intelligently at everything shown and listening with full attention to everything told, ten centibona. And then there were the decorations differing from phalanx to phalanx given for the fun of distinctions.

These were in millicupidon points convertible through Common Measure into centibona, called *mush* in Horde argot, for freckles, bluest eyes, messiest hair, dirtiest feet, *mentula longissima*, silliest giggle, slyest wink, grubbiest fingernails, charm.

Goldenest smile, earliest pubic hair, nautch in the innominata, largest number of warts, longest period between the frumps, slickest kiss, keenest whistle, worst joke, roundest behind, highest pisser, brightest glow from a dandelion under the chin.

A wark in the gaster, a curr in the jaws, and she flies in a figure eight. She bounces in the air, trig of girth and smelling of ginger-flower wax, of apples, of vespa. She thirls her wings, clapfling and brake flip, shimmering her neb. She dips.

He zips in for a squinny, mucin in his ringent jaws, buzzing. She hums. He rimples his golden crissum, sprag for a hump. He brushes her antennae with his forelegs, she his. They dance, a jig, insect of ictus, in linked orbits, more wiggle than step.

Zizz! She pounces, lifts him with all her legs, and flies up. He dangles, wings closed over feet. Over the rose she carries him, through the liliodendron, between the zinnias and sage, peonies, hollyhocks and comfrey, color milling in a quick of sugar.

Amma drew a plan of the world before he created it. He drew the world in water upon the emptiness of space. To draw the egg of Amma you draw a long table of signs and you call this the stomach of all that is. Put a navel at the center. One dot starts all.

Divide the table into quarters, north east south west. Divide each quarter into sixty-four parts. Count them: you have two hundred and fifty-six parts. Add two numbers for each crossline that first divided the table into quarters, and two for the navel.

These are the two hundred and sixty-six things out of which Amma made the world. The quarters are earth, fire, water, air. The crosslines are the *bummo giri*, the eye lines. Four pairs of signs in the quarters are masters of all the other signs of Amma.

X

What works in the angle succeeds in the arc and holds in the chord.

XI

At the Casa da Vinci you could see an owl from Germany, a book of drawings showing the inside of the body, bowels, lungs, a baby in the womb, muscles knit around joints and stretched from bone to bone, a bat, thunderstones, and an egg of the ostrich bird.

You could see the imp Salai, so accomplished a rogue at ten that you could picture his neck in a noose by twenty. Marco had gone at him with a knife and had been thrashed for it by Ser Leonardo himself, who rarely lifted an angry hand. But for Salai, *O già*.

Salai was beautiful. Ser Leonardo was said to be the handsomest man in all Tuscany. *Sono belli tutti i bastardi!* Gian Antonio, as good-natured as a puppy, had been the favorite before Salai, and therefore undertook to deprave him properly and for good.

To discover that he himself was not half as depraved as he thought he was. Human nature, Leonardo said, spreading his hands, is varied. Talents are to be nurtured. Genius in the young is as yet mere energy. Gluttony matures into taste, lust into love.

The pinnace of the *Santa Maria* bore upon Guanahanì on the other side of the world, its banner of Leon and Castille and standard of the Admiral of the Ocean Sea moving in a tossing majesty through strange, crying, wheeling seabirds, fowl of Cathay.

Trumpets, drums, fifes, tabors and pipes sounded a music appropriate to an arrival in China from all the way around the world, a pomp for the procession of dukes toward the queen. The cross was held high on the prow, in triumph, before the scarlet flags.

A little boy the meanwhile in Firenze was drawing a bicycle. He begins with the wheels, turning a compass inexpertly: they are not quite round. Then, with a brown crayon, he draws the spokes, frame, handlebars, seat, sprocket, chain, pedals.

The chain is exactly the same kind as we use now, but Salai does not understand in the drawing he is copying how it is to work. Ser Leonardo's drawing has hachures and fine lines too hard to make. He turns to something easier to draw, a pizzle.

By putting fowl's legs to the balls, he achieves an *uccello*, a bird. He draws another, that smells the rump of the first, as with dogs. He smiles. He laughs. He calls Gian Antonio to come see. *Perche l'uccello di Gian Antonio pende a metà agli sui ginocchi.*

XII

The Greeks called these winged phalloi that Salai drew by the bicycle *pteroi*, seeing the word *eros* in *pteros*, wing. Such poultry are scrawled everywhere in Mediterranean cities, in the sporting houses of Pompeii, the yellow walls of Naples, on Venetian doors.

You could see the design on Corinthian vases in the time of Paul, on bedside lamps in the days of Jonah, and the Florentines still call their members *uccelli*. Gian Antonio took the crayon and drew a supercilious, spoiled face on the page.

He added frogs and points to show that he meant Salai, whose jacket was so decorated. Now, he said, there are three pricks on this page. See the real thing, said Salai. Wait till I get the magnifying glass, and what's this thing with two wheels, pig?

Scrotum of the Pope! Look what you're drawing on. On the other side of the sheet was a round city with concentric walls, towers, galleries, roofed concourses, the kind of thing the *maestro* was forever drawing, whatever the eye of a *strega* they were.

The four pairs of signs which we make in the quarters are the masters of all the others, the Hogon signs. The other signs are of the world. All of this is Amma invisible. The signs are of women and rain and calabashes and antelopes and okra.

They are of things we can see and feel. But inside them all, inside everything, is the great collarbone. Amma is the inside of everything. The world is God's twin. Amma and his world are twins. Or will be, when there is a stop to the mischief of Ogo.

These signs are *bummo*. Two of them, masters of all the rest, belong forever to Amma. The other signs are two hundred and sixty-four. By family, twenty-two. There are twenty-two families of things. Here they are. Listen with sharp ears. First there is God.

The ancestors, the serpent Lébé, that's three, the Binou, speech, the new year at winter solstice, that's six, reconciliation, springtime, the rainy months, that's nine, autumn, and the time of the red sun when the earth is parched and cracked.

Hoeing, that's twelve, the harvest, the smithy, weaving, that's fifteen, pottery, fire, water, that's eighteen, air, earth, grass, that's twenty-one, and the twenty-second is the Nummo, the masters of water with red eyes and no elbows and no knees, like fish.

XIII

Each family has twelve signs, *bummo*, which we cannot see. They are inside the collarbone, in the crabgrass seed. We can begin to see the signs *yala*. These are the corners and joints of things, where you can make a point, where lines meet at an angle.

A dot everywhere a dot can be made in the shape of a thing gives us its *yala*. When you make the *yala* of a thing it has entered being. Its sign is still in the collarbone but it itself has begun to be here in the world. Four dots can define a field.

The *yala* are cornerposts, elbows, knees, the point at which a branch grows out from a trunk. Connect the dots of a *yala* with lines and you have the *tonu* of a thing. Walls connect cornerposts, shin connects ankle and knee. The *tonu* are boundaries and structure.

Fill up the *yala* and *tonu* with wood, with stone, with flesh, and you have the *toy*, the thing itself as we know it, as much as Amma means us to know. For Amma a thing is an example of a plan. The *bummo* is his mind, the *toy* of that *bummo* is our world.

As *bummo* a thing exists as a scratch or wrinkle in the four collarbones rolled into an egg. As *yala* a thing has come into space. With the *tonu* it is given its bones and outline. As *toy* it enters the world, made of Amma's old squandered God stuff.

What a *toy* when Amma connects the *yala* of the stars with *tonu*! All we can make is what God has thought. Matter is alive, has a soul. In the *bummo* there already exist the four *kikinu*, the souls of our bodies, and in them is our life, our *nyama*.

Nor does the life of things depart, however you change their form. The life of each grain of dust lives on in the mud with which we build a house. The *tonu* of mud has assumed the *toy* of house. Still mud, it is also house, *bummo, yala, tonu*. It is part of God.

For is not a house a still animal, needing a soul? What man touches God has first touched. A man's seed is *yala*, the baby in the womb is *tonu*, the baby is born when it has become *toy*. So with seed, plant, and fruit. Nit, caterpillar, butterfly.

Only Amma sees the *bummo* in his four collarbones rolled into a ball, though *bummo* is written in every seed, finer than any eye could ever see. It is written in every crabgrass seed, it is written in the okra, in the spider's eye, in the stars.

XIV

To get to Fourier's grave you go along the avenue Rachel to the Caulaincourt viaduct from which steps lead down to the Cimitière Montmartre. Like Père Lachaise this cemetery is a city of the dead, with tombs for houses along streets with names.

Zola lies here, Eugène Cavaignac, Stendhal, Daniel Osiris, Théophile Gautier, Horace Vernet, Berlioz, Dumas *fils*, and Boum Boum Medrano, of the circus. The leaf-strewn streets are alive with cats who range the tombs and wash their wrists and yawn.

Ask at the lodge and a comfortable registrar in a blue uniform will want to know if you are kin to this Monsieur Fourier. Not by family connection, no. He died when? October 1837. He finds and takes down a ledger from the time of Balzac.

Here we locate the name in menu calligraphy. Someone has written in later *sociologue français*. His address in this mortuary town is 37 avenue Samson, 23rd Division, second row. Cornices and grilles, soot and leaves, medallions, crosses, angels, flags.

We find the tomb, the geometrical figures, the strange words. *La série distribue les harmonies. Let attractions sont proportionelles aux destinées.* He died fallen across his bed, as if he'd knelt to say his prayers before sleep, hands clasped together.

His tribe of cats hissed and slunk away when they smelled death around him. At the funeral there were fellow clerks and neighbors, journalists, economists, sallow revolutionaries and disciples. Charles Gide, weeping, laid late roses on the hands.

Hop, thump, and skitter, little Ogo! The armpit drums talk from beyond the brush. Your big ears are up, capacious as ladles, and you stand on your toes. You are too smart to squeak in your kitten's voice, whistle keen, that is the despair of God.

You imitate the leopard's cricket chirr at the back of your throat. You hear the drums, the blood drums, and you cock your tail and frisk, grinning sideways with impudent eyes that roll upward and laugh, and let your docked tongue hang out for fun.

You laugh as the acacia laughs in the first rainfall after drought. You dance the dance of the stars when they jiggle in the sky, and toss your stringbean hat for sheer wickedness. We know you are there, Ogo. We know you are laughing at us all.

XV

You kick like a zebra, bounce like a hare. Amma looks at you with distress and you chitter in his face. The lightning walks like silver shears opening and closing across the black clouds, and thunder drowns out the ancestor *nummo* drums.

The long wind that burns the desert makes your hair stand backward, but what do you care, Ogo fox, when you can peep with your yellow eyes through the okra and laugh? You break the thread in the shuttle, eclipse the moon, muddy the well.

You clabber the milk, mother the beer, wart the hand, trip the runner, burn the roast, lame the goat, blister the heel, pip the hen, crack the cistern, botch the millet, scald the baby, sour the stew, knock stars from the sky, and all for fun, all for fun.

The darkest and utmost wanderer, five billion six hundred million miles from the sun, the planet Fourier is seven hundred times fainter against the absolute black of infinity than yellow Saturn ringed silver by nine titanic moons, unfindable, unseen.

It is now crossing Cassiopeia as it has been since flags floated through the savage smoke at Shiloh and fifty bugles shrill above a roar of drums loosed the red charge at Balaclava, a speck the size of a midge's eye, a jot of carbon on tar.

It swings so wide afield and so imperially slow that it has been around the sun but four times since Plato was crowned with wild olive at Olympia. It moves backward around the sun, the tenth of the planets and the largest, forever unseeable.

You can see what was most brilliant in the genius of the French at the century's beginning by considering Jacques Henri Lartigue and Louis Blériot as pure examples of its candor and spontaneity. Lartigue made his first photograph when he was six.

He had an older brother to idolize. His father, a banker who liked automobiles and kites, stereopticons and bicycles, was a splendid father. His mother and grandmother were perfect of their kind. The house swarmed with aunts and uncles and cousins.

There were female cousins who dashed down steps and spilled off their velocipedes, male cousins who jumped fully clothed into the mill race. Papa drove a car like the one drawn by Toulouse-Lautrec, the sort you steer with a stick and start with a crank.

XVI

In goggles and dusters, gauntlets and scarves, they tore over the Seine and Loire, scattering geese, making horses rear. The world children inhabit, floating to the moon in a basket launched from the fig tree, is observation that has become perception.

Little Lartigue so loved places and moments that he began to stare at them, close his eyes, stare again, and keep this up until he had memorized a scene in every detail. Then he had it forever. He could summon it again with perfect clarity.

He knew the fly on the windowpane, the mole on a cousin's neck, the skiff tethered to a poplar on the canal. His father saw him at this memorizing, asked what he was up to, told him about cameras, and bought him one to externalize and share his vision.

You took a cork out of a hole in the front of the camera to make an exposure. He stood in his father's joined hands to photograph racing cars zooming by. He followed the racers with a sweep of the camera, getting oval wheels and a forward stretch.

Blériot wept when he saw Wilbur Wright drone up in his Flyer at Le Mans and buzz through figure eights in the blue French summer sky. Blériot's wasplike Antoinette CV flew like a moth and Wilbur Wright's mothlike Flyer No. 4 flew like a wasp.

The persistence of the Antoinette would eventually combine with the agility of the Flyer to become the Spad that Captain Lartigue flew over the trenches of the Marne. When Blériot flew across the Channel in 1909, a man walking a dog saw him land.

The man was Henry James. Did he see the Antoinette glide and cough onto English grass and trindle to a halt? He did not bother to say. Birds come before. The soul, if noble, becomes a speckled bird at death, in ancient belief, or dove or raven.

It rides to the world beyond on the withers of an elk. The pace of this progress is solemn, between red larches and past white water, rocks, wolves in naked light, outposts with lamps and turrets, prophets in booths, structures of the utter continuum.

The rattling yaffle of the silver-stockinged rainbird in its scarlet mutch, the owl's idiot eye, the sparrow's chat and note, the imperial eagle upon its pole: in the ice-age cave in the Lascaux hills there is a bird on a perch to sign a hunter's death.

XVII

Amma the Great Collarbone has put his people the Dogon, their altars, granaries, ancestor tortoises, and trees here in this rocky land so hot, so dry. There are no rivers. For nine months of the year no rain falls. The trees are the baobab and tamarind.

The trees are kahya, flame-tree, butternut, *sa*, jujube, and acacia. At first, from the beginning of time, the Dogon lived in the Mande, before Timbuctoo was there. This homeland was called Dyigou. Then came the men with curved knives, on camels, Islam.

The Dogon brought their altars to Mali. They brought the earth of the first field in baskets and in boats on the Niger. Ogo came with them. That was nine hundred years ago. The earth on which the ark came down they brought to Mali in many baskets.

The forebrain of wasps is built up of a rich tangle of nerve fibers around two quick cups of denser flesh that are like mushrooms of keen mentality and tenacious memory socketed into tissues of casual liveliness and accurate response astride a fat knot.

This central knot seems to be that point around which nature whorls her symmetries. To the right and left of this small brain there stick out like petals the nerves sensitive to light which stream forward and out onto the diamond surfaces of the eyes.

There is yet a third mass of brain that branches down the chest and belly to order the legs, wings, and sting, and to send back the feel of the wind, the wild sweet of coupling, the juicy pull of apple wine, rotten pear mush, the larkspur's velvet nap.

The keenest nerves cluster in the jaws and stomach. The bigger the mushroom cups in the brain, the smarter the insect, for the spies and gatherers among wasps and bees have the deepest cups in their brains of all the foragers, the sharpest eyes.

They discover all and remember all that's useful to their lives. Yellow crumbles, soft meal, gum, grains on the grippers, bright. Green is crisp, gives water, ginger mint keen. Yellow is deep, green is long. Green snaps wet, a wax of mealy yellow clings.

Yellow clings and our jaws crunch green. Crunch curls of dry wood. Cling around green, red shine is the line and red shine is wobble the happy and shimmy the sting. Dance the ripen red, hunch the yellow bounce. Red the speckle, green the ground.

XVIII

The red beyond the red is the finest of the dancers and in that tingle shakes a green. Latch green, brush red. She does no spin for she sucks no wine. We dangle when we suck the wine. She is stronger than the brandy. Red then is the green and red the yellow.

The world in his head, Amma began to make the world. The two hundred and sixty-six *bummo* were written in the collarbone. From himself he took a pinch of filth, spat on it, kneaded it in his fingers, shaping it well, and made the seed of an acacia.

That was the first of all things, an acacia seed. Inside it was the world, all the *bummo*. The filth that Amma brought up from his throat, that is the earth. His spit, that is our water. He breathed hard as he worked, that is fire. He blew on the seed.

That's the air. Then he made the acacia tree on which to hang the seed. Amma then took a thorn from the acacia and stood it point up, like the little iron bell called the *ganana*, the one we ring with a stick, and on this he stuck a lump.

He stuck on it a little dome of acacia wood, so that altogether the two, thorn and dome, looked like a mushroom. Then he stuck another acacia thorn, point down, into the little dome from above. Here he put the two hundred and sixty-six things.

The top thorn he called male, the bottom female. When our children spin their tops they repeat the first dance of the world. How busy is a top, and how still! Amma spun the first world between the thorns, and the seeds of everything were inside.

But — *ah!* — that little dome, as everybody knows, was Ogo's paw. This first world failed that Amma made for us. The dome spun but the things inside went wrong. All the water sloshed out. That's why the acacia tree is both dead and alive, wet and dry.

That is why the acacia is bigger than a bush and smaller than a tree, neither one nor the other, and yet both. It is Amma's first being. It is therefore a person. And yet obviously a tree. It is both person and tree and neither. It is God's failure.

Amma saw that he could not make a world out of the acacia and destroyed it, saving the seed, which contains the plan of all things. Amma began a second time to make the world. For the new world he invented people but he decided to keep the acacia too.

XIX

Miss Stein walked home by Les Editions Budé on the corner of the boulevard Raspail and the rue de Fleurus with its yellow Catulles and Tite Lives in the vitrine that made her think of Marie Laurencin and Apollinaire pink and mauve on the Saint Germain.

Rousseau whom Berenson took to be the Barbizon painter and William James the philosopher who wore Circassian dress as by the Pantheon painted their double portrait using a tape measure to get a likeness, poet and muse, Apollinaire who knew so much.

He could see the modern because he loved all that had lasted from before. You see Cézanne by loving Poussin and you see Poussin by loving Pompeii and you see Pompeii by loving Cnossos. What the hell comes before Cnossos if this sentence is to be a long one?

Alice, what comes before Cnossos, what comes before Cnossos, Pussy? The Musée de l'Homme, says Alice, where Pablo says you can't get your breath, it inspires asthma. On the wall her portrait by Picasso broods and a portrait of Madame Matisse by Matisse.

Madame Matisse in a hat and Madame Cézanne in a conservatory and by Picasso a naked girl holding a basket of roses so glum in her inwardness as to be pouting perhaps for having to pose for Picasso's eating eyes and her bewildering beauty is in her feet.

The little boy Lartigue was just another French scamp to Wilbur Wright if ever they passed on the Haussmann and Wright was but a lean Anglais to Lartigue. She picked up a notebook and wrote: *fact in Cézanne is essence.* Sunlight is always correct.

Wilbur Wright was Ohio and Ohio is flat and monotonous, green and quiet. An so was he, a splendidly tedious man. You cannot be a mechanic and not be tedious, nor the first man to fly and not be green as Ohio is green, nor a hero and not be quiet.

After he flew at Le Mans in figure eights Blériot wanted to kiss him on both cheeks in the French way and the aviators wanted to take him on their shoulders to a banquet but he said that he was too busy and had to make adjustments on his machine.

Wasps in an Ohio orchard, fat black bees in an English garden, butterflies at Fiesole. Wasps drunk on nectar grabble into a yellow umble licorice and lavender, *bourrée* and *gigue*. Ant tells the poppy when to bloom, and sleeping lions make mimosa spread.

XX

Picasso's little girl with a basket of roses has a tender button you can believe and has thrummed it with her grubby finger. She has a good French notion of why big girls whisper and why women sigh. She knows perfectly well why little boys are impudent.

Little boys with their silly spouts and bubbles. She knows why roses ripple round like cabbages and why her name is Rose. Her name is Rose. Fat and intelligent, she sat with her notebooks and pictures around her, brooding and writing and seeing.

Alice was mincing a duck. Outside, to the left, was the Raspail, to the right, the Luxembourg where a captain of artillery first noticed the polarization of light, windows reflecting windows reflecting the level late brilliant winter sun.

On the Raspail she had seen Wilbur Wright looking like a U.S. Cavalry Scout as lean as whang leather. In his keen and merry eyes Paris might have been a country fair, a dream, a postcard from an old trunk. People in Paris are all somehow somebody for sure.

People in Pittsburgh on the other hand are always nobody. But the people in Pittsburgh know who's who. In Paris you don't ever. Sir Walter Scott on the stairs of a hotel asked James Fenimore Cooper if he knew how to find James Fenimore Cooper.

For years she didn't see that and didn't like the painting, it had charm but not the charm of a painting. At Deauville every white and blue building of which is by Boudin you rarely see a barefoot girl except the feet of the Gypsy children naked and brown.

Gypsy children with long innocent brown feet and in the Bois you can see little boys who have terrified their *bonnes* by shedding their shoes but little boys' feet are square and with a knarl of ankle and curled toes but Picasso stops at nothing at all.

There are lovely little girls' feet in Mary Cassatt who came to 27 rue de Fleurus and said I've never seen so many ugly people in all my life, or so many ugly pictures, take me home away from all these Jews, and lovely feet in Degas and yes Murillo.

But they, Degas and Cassatt, were inside painters and kept to the pretense like Henry James that art was art and life was life. Picasso sees all and will paint all in time, even the *inaccrochable,* wait and see, that was next you could be sure.

XXI

Amma began the second world by making the smallest of the grains, the crabgrass seed, in which he put the two hundred and sixty-six things. A *yala*, the corners and turn of things by dots. They are there, in a spiral. Sixty-six of the *yala* are the cereals.

The next four are calabash and okra. The next hundred and twenty-eight are The Great Calabash Round. The last sixty-four are the seed itself, the four collarbones rolled into a perfect roundness. The first six *yala* are male, like the crabgrass.

Three is a male number, penis and testicles. Twin males begin the series. Even Ogo once had a twin. The acacia belongs among the cereals, first of the sixty-six *yala*. But, having *nyama*, a human soul, it is also a person. It is Amma's tree and Ogo's paw.

Wasps in the Baltic amber of the Eocene ran afoul of that pellucid gum eighty million years ago, grave queens eating all of an autumn day against the winter's sleep, fatherless males out foraging in the half light of swamps, worker daughters looking to the young.

The structure of their society in the Eocene is unknown. They enter creation with flowers, and their sharp eyes would have seen the five-toed horse, the great lizards, forests of ferns, daylong twilight under constant clouds and eternal thunder.

How they learned to make paper nests, neatly roomed with hexagonal cells, we cannot begin to know, nor how they invented their government of queen and commoners, housekeepers, scouts and foragers, nurses and guards at the door of the hive.

Ogo. *The white fox of the brush,* Griaule said. He was to have been one of the spirits of time and matter, a *nummo* like his brothers and sisters. In the collarbone, among the thoughts of Amma, he was greedy. He misbehaved in the crabgrass *bummo*.

He bit the placenta of all things. He was looking for his twin before Amma was ready to give him his twin. And then, by nobody's leave, he went on a journey, *to see creation*. Creation, you understand, was still at this time inside Amma's collarbones.

Space and time were still the same thing, unsorted. So before God extended time or space from his mind, Ogo began to create the world. His steps became time, his steps measured off space. You can see the road he took in the rainbow. *To see creation!*

XXII

Amma, Amma! little Ogo squeaked. *I have been to see creation!* Before I have created sun and shadow, Amma cried in fury and despair. Chaos, chaos. *Mischief*. Oh, but Ogo also stole the nerves inside the egg of Amma and made himself a hat to wear.

Ogo's bonnet. They were the nerves with which Amma was planning to make the stringbean. The stringbean is Ogo's bonnet. Not only that, and worse, but he put the bonnet on backwards, for impudence. For hatefulness. To add fun to his Ogo sass.

Amma cut off part of Ogo's tongue for that foolishness. That is why Ogo barks hoarse and high. His pranks nevertheless went on full career. He stole part of the world's placenta, made an ark, and came down to the unfinished world way before he was welcome.

He played God, and havoc. He made things out of the piece of placenta he stole. Look at the plants he made, all in Ogo style: sticktight, mimosa, thorny acacia, *dolumgonolo*, hyena jujube, Senegal jujube, whitethorn, *pogo*, redtooth, *balakoro*, and bombax.

He made crabgrass, indigo, *atay*, cockleburr, arrowwort, brush okra, broomsedge, *tenu*, toadstools, *gala*. And look at them, all, all inedible. He made insects, waterbugs with one side of the placenta, grasshoppers with the other. He made ticks.

He made aphids. He made all these as he was falling through the air, figure eights all the way down. Amma turned the placenta into our earth, and tried to do what he could with the things Ogo created, so that they would fit together somehow, some way.

But the way Ogo made the world was not the way Amma would have made the world. And then there's Dadayurugugezegezene. Spider. She's the old bandylegs who tends to Ogo's spinning, what a pair, and she lives in the branches of the acacia tree.

When Acacia reached the earth in Ogo's ark, it took root, and ended the disorder of the descent, spiraling like a falling leaf, down the birth of space and time. Amma came behind, putting things in place. Acacia is Ogo's world. It is his sign.

Its thorns are his claws, its fruit the pads of his little feet. Like Ogo, the acacia is incompletely made. Like him it searches for its twin. It searches in sunlight the completion of its being. It must search forever, never finding, like Ogo.

XXIII

Leaves fell on Fourier's grave and we thought of the Hordes moving from phalanx to phalanx like fields of tulips. That morning we talked with Fourier's publisher on the rue Racine. We talked about the attempts to build phalanxes in Europe and America.

We told him how the last phalanx in the United States, outside Red Bank, New Jersey, had recently been bulldozed, a large wooden hexagon of a building beautifully covered with kudzu and still inhabitable. The owner bulldozed it rather than sell it.

He would not sell it when he learned that the damned place had been built by Communists. No grand orgies of attractions by proportion and destiny were ever holden to music in its rooms, no quadrilles danced at noon or at midnight there.

No Hordes of children ever set out on quaggas from its gates. About the time this New Jersey phalanstery was sinking into transcendent boredom, having misfollowed Fourier, not quite believing him, German hunters in Africa shot the last quaggas.

The acacia twists in a spiral as it grows. That is its journey. See how its bark is twisted on the bole. See how the branches spiral up. That is the way it spun as it fell in Ogo's ark, turning and turning, casting out the seeds of all other things.

Dada the spider was sent by Amma to set Ogo's chaos in order. Seeing the wild career of Ogo, she decided that he and not Amma would be the landlord of the world. She heard him brag how he had stolen *bummo,* the plan of all creation, from the crabgrass.

What grows, spins. So Dada began a web in the acacia, around and around, *digilio bara vani,* weaving a cone with its point toward the earth. She spins to the right, the acacia in its growth spins to the left. Amma's world is a cone turning opposite a cone.

She spins Ogo's word, which is nothing but the word *move.* The world is atremble, it vibrates, it shifts from one foot to another, it shakes, it dances its dance. It dances Ogo's dance. Did I say he wears his stringbean hat backwards for sass?

Ogo talks with his feet, leaving his tracks in the plan of the ark we draw every evening at the edge of the village. The signs he marks with his paws are the signs we must live by that day. For it is Ogo's gift that he built accident into the world's structure.

XXIV

Mr. Beckett in the Closerie des Lilas lit an Henri Winterman cigar and sipped his Irish whisky. Joyce, he was saying, had first lived somewhere around Les Invalides when he and Nora first came to Paris. They moved, it seemed, every month thereafter.

This was Nora's doing. She was trying to find Galway in Paris, I think. A charming smile softened the hawk's gaze that we knew from photographs. He wore a tweed jacket, old and mended, corduroy trousers, and black turtleneck sweater, and socks.

The socks, we knew, were unusual. His briefcase on the table bore the initials SB above the clasp. Joyce, he said, liked the epigraph from Leopardi on the title page of his *Proust* because *il mondo* could be made to sound like the French *immonde*.

É fango il mondo. The sentiment flowed back and forth from Italian to French, declaring that the world is nasty. We had remarked at Les Invalides that here was the Napoleonic museum in the opening of the *Wake* and the *riverain* of Napoleon's will.

And the concealed *Stephen* in *past Eve and,* and he smiled again at God knows what memories of the alert blind face asking the Greek for this and the Gaelic for that, the ringed fingers tip to tip. He'd a letter from Lucia in England that day.

Jarry with his powdered face had sat in this room, sipping Pernod with the dour Gide. Picasso had sat at these tables drawing caricatures of Balzac and Hokusai. Here Ford and Hemingway corrected the palustral proofs of *The Making of Americans.*

You must understand, Becket said, that Joyce came to see that the fall of a leaf is as grievous as the fall of man. *I am blind,* Ogotemmêli said, opening a blue paper of tobacco with his delicately long wrinkled fingers, his head aloof and listening.

Tobacco gives good thoughts. We are all blind in relation to Amma. You must go into the caves where the contents of Ogo's ark are painted in *tonu.* There are shepherds who will take you. You must see the shepherds when they dance in Ogo's skirt.

They wear the masks and bloody skirts and make the drums speak. I shall never see them again, except in my mind. The dancers come from afar. They have been away for days. They enter the bounds wearing the masks of creation. They wear the granary and the ark.

XXV

They wear the ark of Ogo and the granary of the world and the skirt of the earth bloody from Ogo's rape. We fire the *Frangi* rifles. Our hearts are light, our hearts are gay. It is a funeral and a birth. The eight families of drums begin to beat at dawn.

The Hogon in his iron shoes is with his smiths. The Lébé serpent is to dance for us again. The sun is bright and hot upon the granaries. The altars run with blood. We cry with joy. The calendars are right, the great calendar of the sun, the *yazu* star.

Venus, said Griaule. And, said Ogotemmêli, the calendar of *sigi tolo.* Sirius. Once Ogo had hastened creation and wrecked it, the world needed *uguru.* Another ark had to descend from heaven. All had to be reorganized, redone, reset in their ways, made over.

This was the work of the *nummo anagono,* the catfish. The *nummo* were in the placenta that Ogo had not stolen. They were twins. The mud-wiggler catfish, *nummo anagono titiyayne,* would be the victim, by his own wish, the sacrifice, the redeemer.

He is the beginning of sacrifice. Our altars are in quincunxes because that is the way his teeth fell when he submitted to disintegration. First he was separated from the umbilical cord by which he was attached to Amma in the collarbone.

The cord lay across his penis, which was cut away with the cord. It is now in the sky, the star Sirius, spindle of the world, the pole, the hub. The blood from this severing became the stars. Their spiral is the turning of the world. O greater than acacia!

Greater than Dadayurugugezegezene's work, greater than Ogo's work! The sperm spilt from the testicles of the Nummo became the male waters of wells and rivers and springs and the female water of the sea, the great ax of the rain in its season.

The sperm became the *dugoy* stones which are the twins of the grains, the cowries, and the catfish *anagono sala*. These six things are in the crabgrass seed. The Nummo, to organize the world half made and crazy, circumcised Ogo and made the sun.

The sun is Ogo's foreskin. That is his female twin whom he can never approach, for the fire of the sun is intolerable to be near. As the sign on earth of the sun, the lizard *nay* is Ogo's foreskin. Foreskins are female. It is chaos we slice away in circumcision.

XXVI

When we circumcise we take the chaotic element from the male, the female part of the male. We are born into Ogo's world, and our work is the Nummo's, to organize. We are *nummo* in the womb, an unborn child is a catfish, *anagono*, and when we die.

We are born crazy, full of mischief, like Ogo. From the woman we take her clitoris, from the man the foreskin. The sun is woman, the moon man. Sirius is the center of the sky, and around him there circles a star you cannot make out with the eye.

The center of the earth is the crabgrass seed. Balance of quinces, basket of oranges. Alice, tell me, tell me, Alice, how so settled a soul as I can be so giddy about *la gloire*. About what? says Alice. *La gloire*. You have it, says Alice, whatever it is.

Wilbur Wright flying around the Statue of Liberty and then up the Hudson over all those warships and dipping down to receive the hoot of the *Lusitania's* whistle, *c'est la gloire*. Nijinsky up there at the top of his leap looking like the young Gorki.

You've got flying on the brain, says Alice. Besides, Nijinsky has gone crazy. They say he thinks he's a horse. There is nothing more worthy of admiration to the philosopher's eye, Dr. Johnson said, says Gertrude, than the structure of animals.

What a strange thing for Johnson to have said, says Alice. It is of course architecture that is most worthy of admiration and his not saying so is an example of not seeing architecture. People don't, people who walk take architecture for granted.

They take it for granted because it is good. When everybody has an automobile as in the United States architecture will go all to hell. Architecture is for people on foot. The Chinese had no architecture, nor the Magyars, until they got down off their horses.

There is no architecture in America, never will be. A skyscraper is a city street turned on end. But, says Alice, we drove our Ford through the War. We have seen the trenches of the Ardennes. You have lectured at Oxford and you have lectured at Cambridge.

And at the Wednesday Club in St. Louis. We own Picassos and Cézannes. We have stayed with the Alfred North Whiteheads. Cocteau says he is influenced by you. *It is not enough.* We have passed Joyce and that Frenchman Fargue on the Victor Hugo.

XXVII

The Frenchman raised his hat to us, Joyce did not. He didn't see us. *L'aveugle et le paralytique*, the concierges call those two. It is not enough. We saw the victory parade through the Arc, down the Elysées, O grandest of days, except one other.

ΓΤΑΝΟϹ ΕΡΟϹ ϹΥ ΔΕ ΓΟϹϹΙ
ΤΑΧΥϹ ΤΟ ΔΕ ΚΑΛΛΟϹ
ΟΜΟΙΟΝ

ΑΜΦΟΤΕΡΟΝ

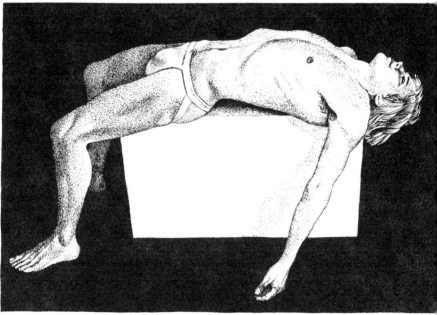

When the *nummo* circumcised Ogo, Amma said: *You should have waited. I could have destroyed him utterly. Now you have mixed his blood with all of creation.* So Amma reversed the spiral of the *nummo*, took the sacrifice, and drenched the world with blood.

Stars began to turn, grain came up, rain fell, wind blew. The fellow traveler of Sirius is the crabgrass seed above, female twin to the crabgrass seed down here. That little star, which many cannot see, unsuspected by some, we know to be the world's granary.

The day after his sacrifice there sprang from the Nummo's blood the *donu*, whose blue wings flash on the Niger in the season of the rains. And the antelope. The Nummo danced as a serpent under our fields. His eyes are red like the first light of the sun.

His skin is green. For legs he has snakes, and his arms are without elbows or wrists. He eats light, and his droppings are copper. But we do not see the Nummo as he is, only his presence in catfish, rain, trees. The Nummo is in the shine of things.

The crabgrass is the granary, the basket the ancestors brought from heaven, the ark of the two hundred and sixty-six things. *It is the menstrual blood.* You have seen wild rams on the rocks near the village at dusk? You have seen a little of the Nummo.

The light in the fleeces of the wild rams is wonderful. You see the Nummo when rain walks in its season from the east, smelling of the river, of green leaves. You see the white of it under the clouds before the first fat drops fall on our red dust.

That is the Nummo. The rain ram. Split a green stick halfway down. Run your knifeblade up each tine so that it curls. That is his sign. You have seen it above the smith's door. Even the French must have seen him in the *yala* of the stars, the Ram.

Between his horns is the sun, the Great Calabash, which is female, the seed basket, the granary, the crabgrass. His horns are testicles, his forehead the moon, his eyes stars, his mouth and his bleat are the wind. His fleece is the earth, the very world.

XXVIII

His fleece is of course copper, which is to say, of water, which is to say, of leaves. When the wind speaks in the leaves and a light like burnished copper dances in the green, and rain falls, that is the presence of the Nummo. His tail is the serpent Lébé.

Lébé danced under our fields when he swallowed his brother ancestor and spat out the *dugoy* stones, the points and junctures of the world. His front feet are the small animals, his hind feet are the big animals, and his *mentula* is the rain.

The granary. It turns in the middle of the air. At the zero point of time its four sides faced the Fish of the Twin Nummo, the Nummo, the Woman with the Grains, and the Nummo with the Bow. Now time is out of kilter, askew, but turning again to zero.

The floor of the granary is round, the roof square, so that the walls rise from their foundation as a cone and find in tapering upward the four creases of the roof's corners. Up each side, in all four directions, there is a long stairway.

The stairway is of ten steps, female on the tread, male on the rise. On the western stairs are the untamed animals, antelopes at the top, and then downward are hyenas, cats, snakes, lizards, apes, gazelles, marmots, lions, and the elephants.

Beside the animals on their steps are the trees in order, from baobab to mimosa, together with all the insects. The tame animals stand on the south steps, chicken, sheep, goats, cattle, horses, dogs, house cats, ancestor tortoise who lives in the yard, mice.

House mice and field mice. On the eastern steps are the birds, hawks, eagles, ospreys and hornbills majestic at the top. Then ostriches and storks. Buzzards and lapwings. Then vultures, chicken hawks, herons, pigeons, doves, ducks, and bustards.

On the northern steps are fish and men. The fish are joined at their navels, like the two fish in the stars. There are four kinds of women, *pobu*, whose wombs are shaped like beans and who have malformed children unfortunate to behold, a grief.

There are women with a vulva like an antelope's foot who bear twin boys, women with a double womb who have twins of different sexes, women with wombs like the crabgrass spiral inside its seed who have twin girls. These are all the kinds of women.

XXIX

There are three kinds of men, men with a short thick *mentula*, men with a *mentula* like a lizard's head, and men with a fine long *mentula*. Our fields are our shrouds. We will be catfish when we die and return to Amma. We are silent at night, lest we stink.

In sixty of Ogo's burrows are hidden the sixty ways of being. We know twenty-two of these: the world, villages, the house for women during their periods, the house of the Hogon, the granary, sky, earth, wind, and animals who have four feet.

Birds, trees, people, dancing, funerals, fire, speech, farming, hard work, cowrie shells, journeys, death and peace. The Nummo's face is leaves and flame. The other thirty-eight ways of being are all that stand between us and Ogo.

They shall be known in time. They are like the young shepherds who have not been seen for weeks in the village, who have gone away in discipline, and who come all unexpected to dance Ogo's dance. Long before they come we hear their drums from afar.

We hear the smith's drum and the armpit drum. The drums speak to the Nummo, for the Nummo. We will have been hearing the drums a long while before we see the young men in their bloody skirts leaping in the first light, wearing Ogo's bonnet.

They wear Ogo's bonnet and pipe in his thin voice. The un-shown things will be revealed to us slowly at first, and dimly, as in a mist at dawn, an awakening and a coming, but suddenly and swiftly at the last, like a loud stormwind and rain.

Everybody was on the streets, men, women, children, soldiers, priests, nuns, we saw two nuns being helped into a tree from which they would be able to see. And we ourselves were admirably placed and we saw perfectly. We saw it all.

We saw first the few wounded from the Invalides in their wheeling chairs wheeling themselves. It is an old french custom that a military procession should always be preceded by veterans from the Invalides. They all marched past through the Arc.

They all marched past through the Arc de Triomphe. Gertrude Stein remembered that when as a child she used to swing on the chains that were around the Arc de Triomphe her governess had told her that no one must walk underneath.

XXX

Her governess had told her that no one must walk underneath since the german armies had marched under it after 1870. And now everyone except the germans were passing through. All the nations marched differently, some slowly, some quickly.

The french carry their flag best of all, Pershing and his officer carrying the flag behind him were perhaps the most perfectly spaced.

The Haile Selassie
Funeral Train

THE HAILE SELASSIE Funeral Train pulled out of Deauville at
1500 hours sharp, so slowly that we glided in silence past the
platform on which gentlemen in Prince Alberts stood mute under
their umbrellas, ladies in picture hats held handkerchiefs to their
mouths, and porters in blue smocks stood at attention. A brass
band played Stanford in A.

We picked up speed at the gasworks and the conductor and
the guards began to work their way down the car, punching
tickets and looking at passports. Most of us sat with our hands
folded in our laps. I thought of the cool fig trees of Addis Ababa
and of the policemen with white spats painted on their bare feet,
of the belled camel that had brought the sunburnt and turbaned
Rimbaud across the Danakil.

We passed neat farms and pig sties, olive groves and vineyards.
Once the conductor and guards were in the next car, we began to
make ourselves comfortable and to talk.

— Has slept with his eyes open for forty years! a woman behind me said to her companion, who replied that it runs in the
family.

— The Jews, a fat man said to the car at large.

Years later, when I was telling James Johnson Sweeney of this
solemn ride on the Haile Selassie Funeral Train, he was astonished that I had been aboard.

— My God, what a train! he exclaimed. What a time! It is
incredible now to remember the people who were on that train.

[108]

James Joyce was there, I was there, ambassadors, professors from the Sorbonne and Oxford, at least one Chinese field marshal, and the entire staff of *La Prensa*.

James Joyce, and I had not seen him! The world in 1936 was quite different from what it is now. I knew that Apollinaire was on board. I had seen him in his crumpled lieutenant's uniform, his head wrapped in a gauze bandage, his small Croix de Guerre caught under his Sam Brown belt. He sat bolt upright, his wide hands on his knees, his chin lifted and proud.

A bearded little man in pince-nez must have seen with what awe I was watching Apollinaire, for he got out of his seat and came and put his hand on my arm.

— Don't go near that man, he said softly in my ear, he says that he is the Kaiser.

The compassion I felt for the wounded poet seemed to be reflected in the somber little farms we passed. We saw cows goaded home from the pasture, gypsies squatting around their evening fire, soldiers marching behind a flag and a drummer with his mouth open.

Once we heard a melody played on a harmonica but could see only the great wheel of a colliery.

Apollinaire could look so German from time to time that you could see the pickelhaube on his bandaged head, the swallow-wing moustache, the glint of disciplinary idiocy in his sweet eyes. He was Guillaume, Wilhelm. Forms deteriorate, transformation is not always growth, there is a hostage light in shadows, vagrom shadow in desert noon, burgundy in the green of a vine, green in the reddest wine.

We passed a city that like Richmond had chinaberry trees in the yards of wooden houses hung with wistaria at the eaves, women with shears and baskets standing in the yards. I saw a girl with a lamp standing at a window, an old Negro shuffling to the music of a banjo, a mule wearing a straw hat.

Joyce sat at a kitchen table in the first compartment to the right, a dingy room, as you entered the fourth wagon-lit counting from the locomotive and tender. His eyes enlarged by his glasses seemed to be goldfish swimming back and forth in a globe. There was a sink behind him, a bit of soap by the faucet, a window with lace half-curtains yellowed with the years. Tacked to the green tongue-and-groove wall was a Sacred Heart in mauve, rose, and gilt, a postcard photograph of a bathing beauty of the eighties, one hand on the bun of her hair, the other with fingers spread level with her dimpled knee, and a neatly clipped newspaper headline: A United Ireland and Trieste Belongs to Italy Says Mayor Curley at Fete.

He was talking about Orpheus preaching to the animals.

— The wild harp had chimed, I heard him say, and the elk had come with regal tread, superb under the tree of his antlers, a druid look in his eye.

He described Orpheus on a red cow of the Ashanti, Eurydice beneath him underground making her way through the roots of trees.

Apollinaire stuffed shag into a small clay pipe and lit it with an Italian match from a scarlet box bearing in an oval wreathed with scrolled olive and wheat a portrait of King Umberto. He tapped his knee as he smoked. He batted his eyes. King Umberto looked like Velasquez's Rey Filipe.

— My wife, Joyce says, keeps looking for Galway in Paris. We move every six weeks.

There came to Orpheus a red mouse with her brood, chewing a leaf of thoroughwax, a yawning leopard, a pair of coyotes walking on their toes.

Joyce's fingers were crowded with rings, the blob of magnified eye sloshed in its lens, he spoke of the sidhe turning alder leaves the whole of a night on the ground until they all faced downward toward China. Of creation he said we had no idea because of the fineness of the stitch. The ear of a flea, scales on the wing of a moth, peripheral nerves of the sea hare, great God! beside the anatomy of a grasshopper Chartres is a kind of mudpie and all the grand pictures in their frames in the Louvre the tracks of a hen.

Our train was going down the boulevard Montparnasse, which was in Barcelona.

— How a woman beats a batter for a cake, Joyce was saying, is how the king's horses, white and from Galway, champing in their foam and thundering against rock like the January Atlantic, maul the sward, the dust, the sty, the garden. Energy is in the race, handed down from cave to public house. Isben kept a mirror in his hat to comb his mane by, your Norse earl eyed his blue tooth in a glass he'd given the pelts of forty squirrels for in Byzantium, glory to Freya.

Apollinaire was showing his passport to a guard who had come by with the conductor. They whispered, head to head, the conductor and the guard. Apollinaire took his hat from the rack and put it on. It sat high on the bandage.

— *Je ne suis pas Balzac*, he said.

We passed the yellow roofs and red warehouses of Brindisium.

— *Ni Michel Larionoff*.

— Whale fish, Joyce was saying, listen from the sea, porpoises, frilly jellyfish, walrusses, whelks and barnacles. Owl listens from the olive, ringdove from the apple. And to all he says: *Il n'y a que l'homme qui est immonde*.

Somewhere on the train lay the Lion of Judah, Ras Taffari, the son of Ras Makonnen. His spearmen had charged the armored cars of the Italian Corpo d'Armata Africano leaping and baring their teeth.

His leopards had a car to themselves.

When we rounded a long curve I could see that our locomotive bore the Imperial Standard of Ethiopia: a crowned lion bearing a bannered cross within a pentad of Magen Davids on three stripes green, yellow, and red. There was writing on it in Coptic.

We passed the ravaged and eroded hills of the Dalmatian coast, combed with gullies like stains on an ancient wall. There was none of us who looked at the desolation of these hills without thinking of the wastes of the Danakil, the red rock valleys of Edom, the black sand marches of Beny Taámir.

From time to time we could hear from the car that bore Haile Selassie the long notes of some primitive horn and the hard clang of a bell.

Moths quivered on the dusty panes, Mamestras, Eucalypteras, Antiblemmas. And O! the gardens we could see beyond walls and fences. Outside Barcelona, as in a dream, we saw La Belle Jardinière herself, with her doves and wasps, her sure signs in full view among the flowers: her bennu tall on its blue legs, her crown of butterflies, her buckle of red jasper, her lovely hair. She was busy beside a sycamore, pulling water out in threads.

— Rue Vavin! Apollinaire said quite clearly, as if to the car at large. It was there that La Laurencin set out for Spain with a bird on her hat, an ear of wheat in her teeth. As her train pulled out of the Gare St. Lazare, taking her and Otto van Waetjen to the shorescapes of Boudin at Deauville, where we all boarded this train, where we were all of us near the umbrellas of Proust, the Great War began. They burnt the library at Louvain. What in the name of God could humanity be if man is an example of it?

Deftly she drew the crystal water from the sycamore, deftly. Her helper, perhaps her lord, wore a mantle of leaves and a mask that made his head that of Thoth, beaked, with fixed and painted eyes.

We were in Genoa, on tracks that belonged to trolleys. Walls as long and fortresslike as those of Peking were stuck all over up to a height with posters depicting corsets, Cinzano, Mussolini, shoe wax, the Fascist ax, boys and girls marching to *Giovanezza! Giovanezza!* Trees showed their topmost branches above these long gray walls, and many of us must have tried to imagine the secluded gardens with statues and belvederes which they enclosed.

He lay with his hands folded over his sword, the Conquering Lion, somewhere on the train. Four spearmen in scarlet capes stood barefoot around him, two at his head, two at his feet. A priest in a golden hat read constantly from a book. If only one could hear the words, they described Saaba on an ivory chair, on cushions deep as a bath, a woman with a bright mind and red blood. They described Shulaman in his cedar house beyond the stone desert it takes forty years to cross. The priest's words were as bees in an orchard, as bells in a holy city. He read aloud in a melodious drone of saints, dragons, underworlds, forests with eyes in every leaf, Mariamne, Italian airplanes.

— An unweeded garden, Joyce was saying, is all an inspired poet rode rickrack the river to usher to us. Her wick is all ears, the lady in the garden. There is an adder in the girl of her eye, dew on the lashes, and an apple in the mirror of the dew. Does anybody on this buggering train know the name of the engineer?

— King's Counsel Jones, cried James Johnson Sweeney.

He had pushed his way between *federales* of the Guardia Civil, Ethiopian infantrymen in tunics and pith helmets, quilted sergeants of the Kwomintang.

I thought of the engineer Elrod Singbell, who used to take the mile-long descending curve of Stump House Mountain in the Blue Ridge playing *Amazing Grace* on the whistle. I remembered the sharp sweet perfume of chinaberry blossoms in earliest spring.

Joyce spoke of an Orpheus in yellow dancing through bamboo, followed by cheetahs, macaws, canaries, tigers. And an Orpheus in the canyons at the bottom of the sea leading a gelatin of hydras, fylfot starfish, six-eyed medusas, feather-boa sealillies, comb-jelly cydippidas, scarlet crabs, and gleaming mackerel as old as the moon.

— Noé, Apollinaire said in a brown study.

— Mice whisker to whisker, Joyce said, white-shanked quaggas trotting *presto presto e delicatamente,* cackling pullets, grave hogs, whistling tapirs.

La Belle Jardinière. We saw her selling flowers in Madrid, corn marigolds, holy thistles, great silver knapweed, and white wild campions. In Odessa she pranced in a turn of sparrows. She was in the azaleas when we went through Atlanta, shaking fire from her wrists.

— Would that be the castellum, Joyce said, where the graaf put his twin sons together with a commentary on the Babylonian Talmud in a kerker dark as the ka of Osiris until a certain lady in jackboots and eyepatch found her way to them by lightning a squally night she had put the *Peahen* into the cove above Engelanker and kidnapped them tweeling as they were sweetening Yehonathan and Dawidh a sugarplum's midge from Luther into the wind and stars but not before twisting her heel by the doorpost and wetting the premises?

— Shepherds! Apollinaire cried to the car, startling us all. We had no shepherds at Ypres. We have no shepherds now.

We were crossing the gardens of Normandy, coming back to Deauville.

Somewhere on the train, behind us, before us, Haile Selassie lay on his bier, his open eyes looking up through the roof of his imperial car to the double star Gamma in Triangulum, twin suns, the one orange, the other green.

Ithaka

THERE WAS, as Ezra Pound remarked, a mouse in the tree. We sat under the *pergola di trattoria* above San Pantaleone in Sant' Ambrogio di Rapallo. His panama on the table, his stick across his lap, Pound leaned back in his chair. In the congenial mat of vine and fig above him there was, as he said, a mouse.

— So there is, Miss Rudge said. What eyes you have, Ezra.

We had been moving Pound's and Miss Rudge's effects from a *dependenza* in an olive grove above Rapallo to the little house that Miss Rudge had lived in before the war and only now had managed to regain. The heavier pieces had gone on the day before. We loaded our Renault named Hephaistiskos with crockery, Max Ernst's *Blue*, the photograph of the Schifanoia *freschi* Yeats writes about in *A Vision*, books, and baskets of household linen.

Pound's cot would not fit into the car and I carried it on my head along the *salita*.

Then we drove down to the harbor, to meet Massimo for a swim. We changed in a *cameretta di spiaggia* that belonged to Massimo's family, Pound into bathing drawers of some black clerical cloth that sheathed him from chest to knee, so that alongside our *piccole mutandine* he seemed to be the nineteenth century, bearded, doctoral, and titled, going swimming with the twentieth. A fierce pink scar, obviously the incision of an operation, curved across the old man's lower back.

— He's going out much too far! Miss Rudge called to me once we were in the water.

She sat under a fetching floppy hat on the terrace of the beach house. It was a while before I saw that she was genuinely anxious.

— Do tell him to come in closer!

I swam out and signaled Steve.

— You and Massimo, I said, swim around the old boy in circles. Don't let him out of your sight.

We had taken the measure of his stubbornness in the last few days. It was phenomenal. He strode ahead of us all up the *salita*, swung himself onto the yacht like a sailor, walked the streets of Rapallo as soldierly as a major general on parade.

They swam around him like dolphins. Miss Rudge kept hailing me back to the pier.

— He won't listen to us, I said. He keeps swimming farther out. I've told the boys not to leave him for a second.

— Tell him to come back!

I didn't want to say I might as well command the Mediterranean to turn to lemonade for all the good it would do, so I raised my eyebrows and looked hopeless. She nodded her understanding but insisted again that I make the attempt.

Meanwhile he was well out into the offing, going great guns, straight out, flanked by Steve and Massimo. I had the awful feeling that their presence merely egged him on.

And at lunch he had been stubborner. We went to a place he had eaten in for years. The waiters made on over him. The proprietor came and shook hands. But when it came to giving an order, Pound fell into his silence. Miss Rudge cajoled. The waiters understood. We kept up a screen of talk to fill in for the silence after the repeated question as to what Pound would fancy for lunch. He would neither say, nor answer yes or no to suggestions.

— Well, then, Miss Rudge said cheerfully, you do without your lunch, don't you, Ezra?

He was anguished, terrified, caught. Then we all became helplessly silent. His head sank deeper between his shoulders. His tongue moved across his lips. He spoke in a plaintive whisper.

— *Gnocchi*, he said.

When I first knew him, years before, at St. Elizabeths Hospital for the Criminally Insane in Washington, he was not yet the immensely old man that I would eventually have to remember, old as Titian, old as Walter Savage Landor, glaring and silent, standing in gondolas in Venice like some ineffably old Chinese court poet in exile, flowing in cape and wide poet's hat along the red walls of the Giudecca.

But in those days his beard and hair were already white. He wore an editor's eyeshade, giving him the air of a man who had just come off a tennis court. He had come instead from a cell. He would have letters from Marianne Moore in a string bag, letters from Tom Eliot, Kumrad Cummings, Achilles Fang, together with a battered and much-scribbled copy of *The Cantos*, and food for the squirrels, who knew him, and ventured close, their necks long with hope, their tails making rolling whisks.

And in those days he talked.

— Billy Yeats, he closed his eyes to say, is most decidedly *not* buried under bare Ben Bulben's head, did you know?

We did not know. He gave us a look that implied that we did not know anything.

— The story goes this way. WBY was parked temporarily beside Aubrey Beardsley in the cemetery for Prots at Roquebrune, up above Mentone, in which place there resided a certain exile from the old sod, her name escapes me if I ever knew it. *When*, therefore, the only naval vessel ever to leave Hibernian territorial waters, a destroyer which I think constitutes the entire Irish Navy, made its way after the war to reclaim Willy's mortal remains, it was met by whatever French protocol and then by the lady exile, who asked the commander if he had an extra drop on board of the real whisky a mere taste of which would make up for centuries of longing for the peat fires in the shebeens, and for the Liffey swans.

— Most naturally he did. Moreover, the captain and crew accepted the lively lady's invitation to her quarters somewhere up the hill between Mentone and Roquebrune, bringing along with them a case of the specified booze.

— Dawn, I believe, found them draining the last bottles. The full litany of Irish martyrs and poets had been toasted at this *festum hilarilissimum*, Lady Circe had danced the fling, the Charleston, and a fandango native to the Connemara tinkers, and the honor guard that was to dig up Willy and bring him with military pomp down the old Roman tesselated steps, presumably with pibrachs squealing and the drum rolling solemnly and without *cease,* and a flag displaying the shamrock and harp whipping nobly in the breeze, were distributed about the lair of the lady like so many ragdolls spilt from a basket.

— Well, and well, some deputation of frog officials turned up, the press had wetted its pencils, and there was nothing for it but that the gallant crew shake a leg, *exhume* Billy Yeats, and mount the distinguished coffin on the prow of the destroyer, where, flanked by handsome Irish guardsmen, it would sail to old Ireland to rest forever, or at least until Resurrection Day, in Drumcliffe churchyard.

— They did, shall we imagine, the best they could. If the ceremony lacked *steadiness,* nothing untoward happened until they had the stiff in the jollyboat headed across the bay. The French Navy boomed a salute and the local *filarmonica* tootled an Irish tune, and well out in the offing but far short of the Irish Navy, the jollyboat, Willy Yeats, and the convivial crew capsized.

— They sank.

— The French, well, the French were *étonnés,* and made haste to fish them *out.*

— But they couldn't find Willy. The Irish were beyond trying, having been drowned two ways, as it were, and the frogs shrugged their shoulders.

— Never mind, they decided. The coffin of state into which they were to put Billy was on board, so they simply moved it up to the prow, hoisted the flag, rolled the drum, and steamed away.

— Billy being still there, at the bottom of the Mediterranean.

Mischief had danced in his eyes. He tied a peanut to a string and dangled it at arm's length. A squirrel ventured toward it, hop a bit, run a bit, stood, and got the peanut loose.

— It's all in knowing how to tie the knot, he had said.

And now the awful silence had found him. Aside from the word *gnocchi* and the observation that there was a mouse in the tree, he had said nothing all day.

The evening was coming on cool and sweet. Our meal was set out on a long table. Pound sat at the head, Steve and I along one side facing Olga Rudge and Massimo. The conversation was about certain experimental film makers, in whom Massimo was interested, Stan Brakhage, Jonas Mekas, Gregory Markopoulas, Smith,

Baille, Anger. Pound plucked the back of a hand already raw.
Suddenly he looked up, glared, and spoke.

— There is a magpie in China, he said, can turn a hedgehog
over and do it in.

His rusted hand lifted his wine to his frizzled beard but he did
not sip.

Massimo shot a glance my way.

— Where in the world did you learn that, Ezra? Miss Rudge
asked.

He put his wine back on the table. He sighed. One hand clawed
at the knuckles of the other.

— I found it, he said, in Gile's dictionary.

Miss Rudge smiled at me.

— We've been reading your Archilochos. Ezra says that you
drew the decorations as well.

The conversation changed over to translation. I tried an anec-
dote about Wilamowitz-Moellendorff and his stout refusal to believe that Sappho was anything but a sound wife and mother of
good family.

— Wilamowitz! Miss Rudge said. He was the handsomest man
in Europe in his day.

— There's a restaurant down in Rapallo, Pound said, where
Nietzsche inscribed the guest book. The *padrone* knew who he
was and asked him to write his name. They still show it. It says:
Beware the beefsteak.

— Ezra, Miss Rudge said, taking a bottle from her purse, it's
time for your pill.

His face fell. She handed him a small tablet.

— Take it with your wine. Right now, so I'll know if you've
had it.

Pound closed his hand around the pill, tight.

— Please, Ezra. What will these young men think? They adore
you. They'll remember these days as long as they live. Do you
want them to remember that you refused to take your medicine?

She did not say that Massimo's father was Pound's doctor,
and that there would be criticism from another quarter if he
didn't take his pill.

Massimo asked about Jack Smith. Pound talked about a pro-
file of Natalie Clifford Barney that some artist had made with a

single hair pasted onto paper. He had found it among his plundered possessions after returning to Italy.

— But it had come unstuck in places and didn't look like her anymore.

— Ezra, have you taken your pill?

He glared at her.

We talked about Sartre's *Les Mots*, which Pound had said he was reading.

— The very beginning is like a page of Flaubert, I said.

— Perhaps, Pound said.

We talked about William Carlos Williams, the Biennale, Greece, Hugh Kenner (*such an entertaining raconteur,* Miss Rudge said), words (*Ezra has been trying to remember the Spanish for* romance), scholars (*It's their wives who are such a trial*), Tino Trova, John Cournos, photographers from *Life* who had run wires all over the apartment in Venice until the furniture looked like the Laocoon, the olive crop, Michael Ventris.

— Ezra, you really must take your pill.

His fist tightened.

It was fully night, and we had had a long day. I asked to be allowed to pay for the meal.

— Never, said Miss Rudge.

No waiter was in sight and I got up to go in search of one.

— No, Miss Rudge said. This is our treat.

She was up and away into the *trattoria* before I could see any sign of a waiter.

As soon as she was out of sight, Pound uncurled his fist and popped the pill into his mouth, washing it down with a swallow of wine.

— Time to hit the hay, he said.

Miss Rudge returned with the *padrone* and his wife. There were handshakes and farewells.

— Ezra, have you taken your pill?

He did not answer. He glared at us all. Both his hands were obviously empty.

We exchanged knowing glances, Massimo, Steve, and I. Miss Rudge graciously did not ask us if he had taken his pill. We did not offer to say that he had. It was a trying moment.

We drove them to the house where Miss Rudge had lived twenty years before, to which she was now returning. We said our good-byes in a room where Pound's cot was neatly made with an American Indian blanket. The pillowcase was of unbleached linen. Ernst's *Blue* stood against the wall.

— *Addio!* he used to say. Now, anguish in his eyes, he said nothing at all.

The Invention of
Photography in Toledo

BITUMEN OF JUDEA dissolves in oil of lavender in greater or lesser densities of saturation according to its exposure to light, and thus Joseph Nicéphore Niepce in the year of Thomas Jefferson's death photographed his barnyard at Chalon-sur-Saône. Hours of light streaming through a pinhole onto pewter soaked asphalt into lavender in mechanical imitation of light focussed on a retina by the lens of an eye.

The result, turned right side up, was pure de Chirico.

Light, from a source so remote that its presence on a French farm is as alien as a plum tree blossoming upon the inert slag of the moon, projects a rhomboid of shadow, a cone of light. A wall. A barn. Geese walking back and forth across the barnyard erased themselves during the long exposure.

Foco Betún y Espliego, the historian of photography, spends several pages sorting out the claims of Friedrich Wilhelm Herschel and Nicéphore Niepce to the invention of photography and decides that the issue cannot be resolved without more evidence. Herschel, the discoverer of The George Star which Fourier the philosopher and Joel Barlow, in his unfinished epic on the Erie Canal, called the planet Herschel, and which is now known as Uranus.

A small town safe in its whereabouts, Titus Livy said of Toledo. It sits on a promontory at a convergence of rivers.

Has not a silver cornet band strutted down its streets in shakos and scarlet sashes, playing with brio and a kind of melancholy elation *Santa Ana's Retreat from Buena Vista?* Swan Creek flows through its downtown into the blue Maumee, which flows into Lake Erie. It bore the name of Port Lawrence until Marcus Fulvius Nobilor erected the *fasces* and eagles of the SPQR in 193. Originally a part of Michigan until Andrew Jackson gave his nod to Ohio's claim, the fierce violet of its stormy skies inspired El Greco to paint his famous view of the city. It was in Toledo that the Visigoths joined the church and made Spain Catholic. And in 1897 Samuel L. (Golden Rule) Jones was elected mayor on the Independent ticket. Its incredible sunsets began to appear in late Roman eclogues.

When the summer is green with grasshoppers and yellow with wasps, the shining Tagus slips under its arched bridges around the three sides of Toledo. The house were photography was invented sits on a Roman base, its walls are Celtiberian, its windows Arab, but its rooms, for all their Moorish tiles, holy cards, and paralytic furniture from the age of Lope and the hidalgos, are bravely modern.

Édouard Manet visited this house on his trip to Spain during which he almost starved owing to an inability to force a bite of Spanish cooking upon his Parisian palate. In fact, he called onto the field of honor a man who asked for a second helping of a dish that he found particularly revolting. Manet assumed that the man was offering him a deliberate insult.

A radio that looks like a French cake with dials comes on at dusk when the powerhouse sends a thrill of electricity through all the wires of the city and small orange bulbs light up in pink glass shades and the radio sizzles *The March of the Toreadors,* a talk by a priest on the oneness of our spiritual and political duties, a lecture by a Major Domo of Opus Dei on the plague of heresies that besets the French, and a piano recital by Joaquin Turina, playing furiously into a microphone in Madrid that looks like a Turkish medal worn only by field marshals who can claim collateral descent from the Prophet.

There is a room off to the side of the house where photography was invented where you can look into a microscope and see cheesemites doing the act of nature if you are lucky. Some are of the opinion that this imperils one's soul, and others, more enlightened, maintain that it is educational.

— It is so French, you will hear.

— It is Darwinian, you will also hear.

— The Pope has given his blessing to photography. A maiden can send her photograph to her swain and thus spare herself the indecency of a personal encounter. You can go to the photographer's studio and choose a picture that most resembles your son who has gone to the front and have a likeness to put on his grave when the government sends his body home on the railway.

El Caudillo has sat for his portrait many times.

All the world loves a big gleaming jelly.

Napoleon as he was consummating his marriage to Joséphine was bitten in the butt by her faithful dog at, as he liked to relate to intimate friends, the worst possible moment. Real life, said Remy de Gourmont, makes miserable literature, and even Balzac would not have known what to do with such an unmanageable a detail. It is simply appalling. But real life is all that photography has.

Betún y Espliego in the course of compiling his monumental history of photography sifted through thousands and thousands of tintypes and daguerreotypes to find the patterns of attention and curiosity into which this new art fell. He reproduces in his work a photograph of a man standing on a Berlin sidewalk with Einstein. Einstein didn't know the man from Adam's off ox. The man had stopped Einstein and asked permission to be photographed beside him on a Berlin sidewalk.

— It is, Einstein conceded, a simple enough request.

A photograph of Lenin reading *Iskra* at a Zürich café accidentally includes over to the left James and Nora Joyce haggling with a taxi driver about the fare. A Philadelphia photographer made several plates of paleolithic horse fossils at the Museum of Natural History. In one of the pictures two gentlemen stand in the background, spectators at the museum. One wears a top hat and looks with neurotic intelligence at the camera. He is Edgar Allan Poe. The other gentleman is cross-eyed and wears a beret. God knows who he is.

Betún y Espliego, at the time of his degree from the Sorbonne, explained in a lecture that for the first time in the history of art the accidental became the controlling iconography of a representation of the world.

There are no photographs of Van Gogh as a grown man except of the back of his head. This image occurs in a photograph of a man of some importance now forgotten. But we can identify the figure with its back to the camera as Van Gogh.

There is a photograph of the ten-year-old Vincent. Picasso says that there is a strong resemblance to Rimbaud. A classmate of Vincent's who survived to a great age remembers his hundred freckles across the cheeks and nose, and that the color of his curly hair was bright carrot. Note, says Betún y Espliego, how the accuracy of the photograph had in this instance to be supplemented by an old man's memory.

When the photograph was invented in Toledo the Indians came into town and sat for their portraits. It was the only interesting thing the white man had come up with in all these years.

A photograph of Socrates and his circle would simply look like an ugly old man with bushy eyebrows and the lips of a frog. The homespun texture of his wrinkled tunic would probably be the most eloquent part of the photograph, as the eyes would undoubtedly be lost in shadow. Which of the gangling, olive-skinned young Greeks around him is Plato? The one with pimples and sticky ringlets across his forehead? Which is Xenophon? Who is the woman stabbing a hex of two fingers at the camera?

Skepticism has no power whatever over the veracity of a photograph. It is fact and is accepted by all minds as evidence. The Soviets have gone through all their photographs of the revolution and erased Trotsky. They have put Stalin at Lenin's side even when he was a hundred miles away eating borshch. Since the invention of the photograph we have ceased to dream in color.

On the door of the house in Toledo where photography was invented La Sociedad de la Historia Fotográfica placed a brass plate in 1934. Betún y Espliego made a speech. Ohio, he said, is a paradise on this earth. He alluded to the blue Susquehanna, to the sweet villages where, as Sarmiento said in his *Viajes*, there is more material progress and more culture than in all of Chile and Argentina combined.

An exhibit of photography in historical perspective was mounted that year in the Louvre. The spectators saw photographs of Ibsen walking in the frescade of a Milanese garden, his hands behind his back, Corsican gypsies around a campfire, Orville

Wright shaking hands with Wilbur Wright before they flipped a quarter to see who would make the world's first guided flight in a craft heavier than air, Sir Marc Aurel Stein on the Great Wall of China, Jesse James playing a Jew's harp, T. E. Lawrence entering Damascus under the banners of Allah, The Empress Eugenia saying her prayers, Carnot and the Shah of Persia going aloft in a balloon, La Duse reclined on a wicker chaise, Ugo Ojetti and his mama, ladies of fashion kneeling in the street as the Host passes (the Sicilian brass band looking strange beside priests in embroidered robes), Neapolitan convicts going down long stone stairs, emigrants filing through a Roman arch on their way to the boat train and Ellis Island, Allenby making a Turkish band play *The Crescent of Islam Moves Like a Scythe Across the Infidel* into a telephone held by a Sergeant Major of the Royal Welsh Dragoons, Queen Victoria extending a finger to an Irish member of Parliament.

In 1912 Betún y Espliego abandoned his history of photography to devote his life to getting a clear picture of the Loch Ness Monster. The last photograph we have from his hand is a group portrait of the Royal Scots Greys posed with His Imperial Majesty Nikolai II, Colonel of the Regiment. It is an early example of color photography, and the Tsar's face is rusty orange, his beard kelp green. All the hues of the plaids are wrong, and the Elders of Edinburgh therefore refused to allow the picture to be exhibited in the Castle, though George V looked at it privately, and the Metropolitan of Moscow and Neva had one framed in silver and rubies for the high altar of SS. Boris and Gleb.

Betún y Espliego suffered awful loneliness in his vigil on the gray shores of Loch Ness. The bagpipes ruined his kidneys, the porridge his stomach. The religion of the locals seemed to be some revolting kind of speculative philosophy.

His wife Lucinda came to the edge of Scotland and shouted over the wall that he was to come home immediately to Madrid. Franco and the Falangistas were at the gates of Barcelona. Their children wept the large part of the time. She had not heard a string quartet in six months. Was this place, she shouted louder, the land of the Moors?

Wasps the meanwhile built several phalansteries in a china cabinet and the three corners of a ceiling in the house where pho-

tography was invented in Toledo. Young wasps practiced clap-fling and flip around the twenty-watt bulb of the electric light, and the queen of the colony droned in courtly splendor above the radio, the sound of which she took to be a fine summer storm.

There was no darker moment, a voice said from the radio, than when man fixed images of grandmothers and wars on paper with nitrate of silver, the pylons of Luxor and herds of buffalo, no profounder undoing of the spirit, so that the Spanish people must now see the savages of utmost Africa in all their immodesty, Protestant women in dresses that leave bare their ankles and elbows for all the world to see, zeppelins blooming into a cloud of fire, battlefields, refrigerators, and bicycles, leaving the unseen and invisible realities of devotion and meditation in that realm of the mind where the sleep of reason breeds monsters.

A little boy whose hair was a gorse of snarled rust and whose eyes were as blue as an October sky snuck one day as close as he dared to the caravan where Foco Betún y Espliego lived on constant lookout for the Loch Ness Monster. It was a morning when Betún had set up his camera on a tump of daisies and was under the black cloth, the sensitized plate ready in his hand, peering out through the lens at the waste waters that lay as still as a sodden carpet under a desolation of clouds.

— Och, said the bairn from a distance, ye're nae a ceevilized mon t' be sae enthralled by that trippid bonnet.

For response there was a swarthy hand waving him away from under the cloth.

— Rest ye easy, said the boy. I wadna coom closer for a great jool.

One day the boy brought the free-kirk minister, who had heard of photography, a French and frivolous art. He shouted his opinion that it would come to nothing. On another, he brought the laird of the manor and his two daughters. He charged a farthing a head for the service. Their parasols and curls danced in the wind, and the laird pronounced Betún an idiot.

— It's the munster lurks in the loch he's sae still aboot, the bairn explained to the laird.

On a spring day in 1913 the monster, *Nessiteras rhombopteryx*, a plesiosaurus with lots of teeth, saw Betún as clearly as his Jurassic vision allowed, an insect with five feet, black wings, and one large eye that caught the sun with a fierce flash. As a detail of the Out There, Betún held little interest, and until he came into the Here he would not eat him.

Betún's photograph shows a long wet nose and lifted lip, an expressionless reptilian eye, and a gleaming flipper. It was published in *La Prensa* upside down and in the London *Times* with a transposed caption identifying it as the Archduke Franz Ferdinand arriving in Sarajevo for a visit of state.

The Antiquities of Elis

ON THE MOUNTAIN road from Olympia to Elis you come to the ruins of Pylos. White dust, which the traveler to Greece must learn to endure, had covered my mule and my baggage, the beard and eyebrows of Pyttalos my guide, and the copper hair of Lykas my courier. It was late summer, the crickets trilled all day, there was a bronze tone in the green of the Elean forests, and Pyttalos, whose face was more wrinkled than any I had even seen, said in his offhanded way that we were in a place known to be bad for werewolves. I took him literally at first, Greeks are apt to say anything, and then I saw he was making some allusion to Lykas, whose name of course means wolf. I looked to Lykas for an explanation, or for the joke, but he was grinning as always, as good-natured as a dog.

— What do the werewolves do? I asked.

— Eat lambs, Pyttalos said. Flatten girls and wives.

I shook dust from my sleeves, observed the varieties of nettle, star flower, asphodel, and briar, and said that Lykas hadn't bitten us yet.

Pyttalos looked surprised. He put up well with my foreign ways and astounding ignorance, though I had overheard him explaining my importance, and hence his, at Olympia. I was, he said, taking Hellas down in a book, so that the Roumeli and Calabriani could know its shrines and holy places. I asked as many questions as a philosopher, he elucidated, but was not so womanish or thick in the head.

— Not Lykas, Kyrie. Werewolves. Lykas is I should think a Bear brother, and says his prayers to Apollo Wheat Mouse, and

[131]

still goes to the equinoxes with his mama. You have to belong to the Lady to get on the road you go off of into the wolf spell.

Lykas picked up a flint and shied it at a lizard.

— I've been to the Artemis service, he said. With my sister.

— Pylos, Pyttalos said, pointing.

The ruins of a wall ran in and out of wild olive across a white riverbed, the Ladon when the winter rains make it into a river again.

— Two rivers, Pyttalos explained. Over to the left is the Peneios. The Ladon comes into it just where the old town used to be.

I was told in Elis that this Pylos was named for its founder Pylon Klesonides, that Herakles destroyed it, that the Eleans rebuilt it, but that it never amounted to anything, and has been abandoned for a century or more. They also remarked that it is the Pylos of Homer. They could be right, for the river Alph flows through Elis, and there is no such river among the Pylians on the coast across from Sphakteria, and no one has ever heard of a Pylos in Arkadia.

Before setting out for Elis we had eaten honeycomb and goat cheese under the great oak by the sanctuary of Artemis of the Mating Dance, where the bones of Pelops lie in a bronze box. Mount Sipylos is said to be the home of that licentious and sacred dance, and Pyttalos laughed, licking honey from his fingers.

— Some dance, he said. These Eliskoi have a house for the Lady every hilltop and ash grove. I've seen the dance at the Thargely and by the Dog there wasn't a bird on its nest.

Lykas chewed his barley cake and grinned.

We had been on the road for two days when we came to the ruins of Pylos. Aside from werewolves, which Pyttalos assured us appeared there at the right time of the moon, Pylos had nothing to offer but her overgrown ruins, and we pushed on to Herakleia, an Elean village on the river Kytheros. There is a spring outside Herakleia inhabited by the nymphs Kalliphaeia, Synallasis, Pegaia, and Iasis, or Shine, Leap, Gush, and Heal. Together they are called the Ionides, named for Ion the son of Gargettos, who came here from Athens. The spring is particularly efficacious in curing arthritis and rheumatism. Pyttalos remarked that it took a poultice of asafetida and horseradish to get at the root of his aches, and that he left sitting in a cold spring to the young and the not overly bright. And added that it was scarcely decent anyway.

We had an onion and some hot wine with sage in it at Herakleia, and looked at the sanctuary of the nymphs, scaring a heron as we approached. I admired the butterflies and lizards, Pyttalos found a trefoil which he picked, and we moved on toward Letrini.

There is little left of Letrini. A few houses still stand, and a temple of Artemis Alpheiaia. Alpheios, the legend goes, loved Artemis, and decided to carry her off. The goddess had come to Letrini for her night festival, to dance under the full moon with her virgins. She knew Alpheios' intent, and she and her companions smeared their faces with river mud, so that Alpheios could not tell which of the dancers was Artemis. I think rather that the temple is to Artemis Elaphiaia, Artemis of the Deer Folk, whose cult is observed at Elis. And yet the Eleans say that Elaphios was Artemis's childhood nurse.

The muddy face of Artemis was probably a misunderstanding of some rite now lost, some drama perhaps with masks, or some disguise of the goddess far more serious than a device to avert the lust of a river, and who knows what allegory, what sacred poem, lies behind that?

Elis as we approached it on its mountain plain was all honey, white, and green along the Peneus, which flashed crystal in its crooked course. The squares and oblongs of houses and temples were scattered without order among trees. The Greeks, who have such an eye for symmetry, like to dispose their buildings at odd angles, to show that geometry may please but not tyrannize. I saw instantly that I was coming to an extraordinary country town. All the grandeur of the Olympic games was at Olympia itself, which in its monumentality and profusion of statuary seemed more Egyptian than Hellenic. Elis, where the athletes trained and qualified for the games, and where the judges resided for most of each year, was elegant and relaxed. The sun had bleached and mellowed it. Athletes, trainers, and officials from all over the civilized world gave it a cosmopolitan touch, and yet as soon as we were in its streets, among poultry, dogs, farmers, old women with baskets of squash, and scholarly men with books under their arms, I saw that its identity was inviolate, peculiar to itself, rich of tone.

Our innkeeper cocked his ear, as if he were going to hear Scythian. We had come from Olympia, *yes?* His *rho* was more liquid than Pyttalos's and his use of the dative smacked of Athens. A chicken and a dog watched us unpack the mule, in hope of something dropped.

Asses brayed throughout the night, as in every part of Greece, the bronze trumpet of the Fury Megaira. Crickets chirred, the nightingale trilled, two owls called to each other from distant trees. In the false dawn all the cocks of Elis crowed.

We rose late, the privilege of travelers, dipped fresh bread in hot wine, fought the bees from our honey, and sampled a plate of figs which the innkeeper's wife, a provincial Hera, brought us as a token of esteem. I was, she had heard, writing the picture of Elis for the Romaioi. I looked at Pyttalos without catching his eye. Would I mention the inn, its moderate prices, its desire to accommodate the better sort of traveler? I do. It is the Xenodokheion Hermes on the Hodos Marathonos. The straw is clean, the wine salubrious, the bread excellent.

Lykas had put on a fresh tunic, Pyttalos had appeared with his staff, and we set off to see Elis.

The old gymnasium was the principal object of my visit, and we went there first. It is here that the athletes train before they go to Olympia. There is much about it that reminds me of all schools. Like my Lydian grammar school, it has a sweet quietness and intimacy which I missed at the Academy. It has the spiritual clarity of beginnings.

Tall plane trees line the tracks inside the wall that rings the Xystos, where Herakles himself once pulled up thistles. These are the training tracks. The races for the competitions are run on the Sacred Course, which is also within the walls.

Inside the gymnasium is the Plethrion, or wrestling floor, a hundred feet square. Here the Hellanodikai match the wrestlers by age, weight, and ability. A group of boys stood gravely around a trainer near a door at the far end of the gymnasium. Along a wall stand altars with statues. First there is Herakles Parastatos of Ida, before which the boys take the military oath of comradeship. Then there is a statue of Eros and beside it the god Anteros, or Love Returned, the principle by which boys in love with each other do not act like boy and girl, but sustain decency and chastity in their friendship. Beyond Anteros are statues of the Barley Mother and her daughter whom we may not name.

There is no statue here of Akhilleus, or altar. An oracle forbade it, but there is a cenotaph outside where on the equal day and night at the end of summer the Elean women cover their heads with their shawls, bare their breasts, and wail for the son of Peleus and Thetis.

A smaller gymnasium near the larger one is called the Cube, for its shape. It has a wrestling floor and a boxing ring. We saw the soft gloves hanging on pegs, and the strapped pouches with which the boxers were girded. Opposite the door stood a Zeus bought, as was inscribed on its pedestal, with fines paid by Sosandros of Smyrna and Polyktor of Elis.

There is a third gymnasium, for beginners, called the Moltho, or soft floor. Here we found a head and shoulders of Herakles in bronze, and a relief built into the wall showing Eros as an athlete holding a palm branch which Anteros, also an athlete, is trying to take from him, illustrating the balance and tension of comradely love, as they both wish to be the giver. The bow and the string cannot pull the same way.

On each side of the door to this third gymnasium there is a statue of the boxer Sarapion, who was born in the Alexandria which faces Pharos in Egypt. He brought wagons of wheat to Elis in the time of the famine, and one of the statues honors him for that. The other honors him for winning the crown of wild olive at the two-hundred-and-seventeenth Olympiad. The third gymnasium is also used for the recitation of poetry and oratory. The room set aside for this is called the Lalikhmion, after the man who had it built. Round shields painted with the signs of tribes hang around the walls.

The way from the gymnasium to the baths, cobblestoned and strewn with leaves, is called the Silent Road, and here we came to the sanctuary of Artemis Friend of Adolescents, Philomeirax, whether from her being the neighbor of the gymnasium or from a cult of olden time which eventually begat the gymnasium, the baths, the tracks, I do not know. The name of the road was explained this way: once the infantry of Oxylos was curious to know what went on in Elis, and by this road their spies came to listen at the wall, so silently that no one heard them.

I wonder if in times now forgotten the city cult was that of Artemis Philomeirax and the silence not that of Aitolian spies but of initiates whose procession came along this road to the rites.

The stone road was dusty, quiet, and slowly covering with leaves. Here a thistle had come up between stones, its leaves curled and ornate; there, a stray flax flower. The plane trees were old and tall, and we relished their shade and peacefulness. Pyttalos had been here many years before, and remarked that it was all the very same.

Three boys came onto the road from the smaller gymnasium, the Moltho, going to the baths. Their chests rose and fell, and they breathed through their mouths. They were wrestlers, for ovals of dust spotted their oiled bodies. One had thrown a khiton over his shoulders, one wore a triangle of white linen knotted at each hip, the other was naked except for a blue ribbon around his forehead. Their hair seemed to have been cut with the bread knife. They looked at Lykas, in the manner of boys and dogs, thinking perhaps that he was someone new at the schools. He blushed.

The temple was very old. Its northern side was black with lichen, and the sun and rain had bleached its eastern wall to the whiteness of ancient bone. The statue of Artemis was carved of olive wood in the archaic style. Her face was covered with beaten gold so impure as to be red. She wore a stole of bright but countrified needlework, mere geometry to indicate blue stars, a white moon, a yellow sun with its rays, and a row of partridges. The cult statues were equally primitive and equally blunt, a girl with a rather overstated notch to emphasize her place in nature, and a boy with broad shoulders and copious testicles. The interior was dim—we looked through the latticework of the door—and smelled of clean old stone and still, dry air. The figures were serene in their half-light, except for the golden mask of Artemis, which had the strict kindness of the Spartan women written on it in, so to speak, the Elean dialect. Before the altar there were terra-cotta figures, no larger than toys: horses, deer, birds, bears, lions.

These sweet temples which I have seen everywhere in Greece, her islands and colonies, with their thin, fluted columns browned by age and sunlight, with their trees, knot-kneed or mossy or slender still in their fortieth year, gather all their circumjacence, their rocks, nettles, narrow windows, god images, turning shadows, birds' nests, wasp hives, urns, priests, and acolytes, into a venerable family, for how can a tree's shadow, flowered, full-leaved, or laden with snow, move on a temple's wall from the old age of Herakles to the graying of Hadrian's beard, without becoming its sister or brother as those kinships stand among wood and stone? It was Herakleitos who said that some things are too slow to see, such as the growth of grass, and some too fast, like the arrow's flight. All things, I have often thought, are dancing to their own music. A Lydian song is soon over, but the music to which the zodiac is turning requires twelve times three thousand years to close its harmony, if we may follow the calculations of Pythagoras, and the rhythms of time for a child are so much slower than for a man that we have lived for centuries before our beards arrive. It is the young who are so very old. Yet there is a mortality even in children which we cannot discern in old temples, which, in surviving generation after generation, have taken on that grace by which their sacredness shall probably survive Greece and Rome. Earthquake and impiety cannot destroy them all.

There are two roads from the gymnasiums to the agora. One goes by the cenotaph of Akhilleus to the quarters of the Helleno-dikai. It is along this road before sunrise that you can see the trainers and runners coming down to the tracks. The other road goes by residences and gardens.

The place and market at Elis are not laid out in the Ionian manner, but have kept the old style roofed columns, with pas-sageways between, as congenial as the eastern markets, or the shaded and comfortable back-streets of Athens and Corinth. We were amused to learn that they call their market the Hippodrome, for they tame horses here as well as buy and sell, talk and play checkers. The portico facing south has Doric columns, stately and plain. Here the Hellenodikai can usually be found passing the time of day. We were shown altars that can be moved about in the market, permanent ones being inconvenient in so busy a place. The Hellenodikai have rooms off the marketplace, and live here for ten months of their term. They take instructions in the games from the judges, and decide which athletes are to be pitted against each other in all the contests.

Across the street from the portico of the Hellenodikai is the

Korkyrean Portico, built with money from the raids on Korkyra
in the time of the wars with that island. This series of roofed
columns has a wall down the middle, with statues set against it,
one of which is of the philosopher Pyrrhon, who would admit
nothing. That a room might be empty, he could never subscribe
to, for the predication was too fraught with ambiguities to be
considered. Empty of light, it was full of dark. Empty of chairs
and tables, it was full of air. Pyrrhon is buried outside Elis, at a
place named the Rock, and we walked out to see his tomb. The
Rock was once a town, but there is nothing there anymore.
Pyrrhon's sarcophagos, along with some others, lies in tall grass
near a grove of pine trees.

How old the world!

Another statue in the market at Elis is of Apollo Doctor, the
same Apollo you find at Athens. There is also a Sun of stone, with
rays coming from his head; and a Moon, with horns.

At the end of a wide street off the market is a grove of terebinth
and manna ash where a delicate and elegant sandstone sanctuary
of the Graces stands in a lace of shadow. Their statues are wooden,
their robes gilded, their heads, hands, and feet of white marble.
One holds a rose, Aphrodita's flower; another, a sprig of myrtle,
sacred to the rites of Aphrodita and Adonis. The third holds a
pair of dice.

Beside the Graces stands an Eros, also of wood.

Farther on, there is a temple of Silenos, interesting in that it
is not to Dionysos and Silenos but to Silenos alone. His image is
fat and rampant. A satyr is offering him a cup of wine. It is sad
to know that satyrs are mortal. I have seen the tomb of one in
the land of the Hebrews, though I could not read his name or
age on the red stone. A learned man of their tribes showed it to
me. When I told him that the forests of my native Lydia, and of
the Greeks, were as full of satyrs as the streets of Damascus with
camels, he smoothed his black beard and made no comment.

There is also a satyr buried at Pergamon.

In the marketplace there is also a kind of temple, a roof over
pillars carved of oak, but with no walls. It is, the Eleans say, a
tomb; whose, no one can remember. An old man told me that it
was the tomb of Oxylos, but could say no more about it.

Near this forlorn structure is the House of the Sixteen, where select women weave the annual robe for Hera. Its yard is surrounded by a wall, and inside that by several large chestnut trees.

At the edge of the market there is a temple in ruins, with only its pillars still standing, roofless and bereft of statuary. Tall grass mixed with wild flowers grows around it, and the inside, naked of altar or images, was alive with crickets and lizards when I looked. It was in its day dedicated to the Roman emperors. I daresay it dates from the vanity of Nero Augustus, whose opulent hand touched Greece with its fever. Hadrian, who was emperor until my eighteenth year, was already beginning to shy away from the idea of divinity inhering in a living man; the second Antonine was too religious to encourage a cult of the emperor, and Marcus Aurelius has refused altogether to assume the title Divus.

Behind the arcade of the Korkyrean spoils there is a temple to Aphrodita of the Sky. Her image of ivory and gold is by Pheidias, and stands with one foot on a tortoise. Beside this temple is a walled grove for the Common Aphrodita. Her statue is in an underground room, a bronze Aphrodita riding on a bronze billy goat. The sculptor is Skopas, and his worldly Aphrodita on her randy buck is as well wrought in its manner as the etherial Aphrodita of Pheidias. I do not know the meaning of the tortoise.

The Eleans are the only people who have a temple to Hades. It is opened once a year, only the priest is allowed inside, and the reason is this. When Herakles was besieging the Pylos whose ruins we saw on the road from Olympia, Athena came to help him. In those days Hades had a temple at Pylos and came to the defense of the city. If Hades found his worship at Pylos acceptable, the Eleans felt that his rites ought to be established in Pylos's mother city Elis.

There is also a temple for Fortuna at Elis. Her image is enormous, and stands outside the sanctuary proper. It is of gilded wood, but the face, hands, and feet are of marble.

To the left of this temple is a small shrine to Sosipolis. The painting inside is of a dream. It depicts Sosipolis as a boy in a blue robe on which stars are painted. He holds the horn of Amaltheia. I saw no image of him as the sacred serpent, or with Ilithyia.

There is a statue of Poseidon in the residential part of Elis. He is a beardless young man with crossed legs, leaning with both hands on a spear. He is dressed by the Eleans in a tunic of linen, over which there is a flaxen khlamys and a cloak of wool. This is Poseidon of Samikon in Triphylia, brought here as a trophy. The Eleans say that it is an image of Satrapas, one of the names of Korybas, and not Poseidon at all. Poseidon to the inland Greeks is the Earth Shaker; to the Greeks of the islands and ports he is a god of the sea. Pyttalos, indeed, said that Poseidon is the god of walls, and it was his opinion that this dressed statue was of an Olympic victor, and that a gaggle of religious widows and wives with nothing better to occupy their time had set it up here to add awe and flash—here he made a curious sign with his hand, probably obscene—to the neighborhood.

The houses hereabout had walled gardens and were set among trees. I saw a splendid wild red of late roses through a gate, with a fall of petals beneath the bush and their musk loose in the air. There was also an old herm from the time of Alexander, and a sundial. Through the inner gate I could see Persian chickens in a yard, and a cart horse gone white around the muzzle munching fodder from a rick.

On the acropolis there is a temple to Athene, quite fine. The statue is of ivory and gold, the work of Pheidias, if we may believe the Eleans. A cock stands on her helmet, the emblem of her warlike genius, or perhaps the symbol of Athene the Worker.

Along the cobbled road from the market down to the River Menios we went through an old part of the town where the houses are close, the most of them being over the workshops of sandalmakers, ironmongers, smiths, potters, and dyers. We stopped to admire the crocus yellow of a cauldron of boiling willow twigs. There were cats sitting in almost every window along this busy street, and dogs and children at every door. There was even a tame owl sitting on a girl's shoulder, against which Lykas made a hex, spitting into his fingers and touching his forehead and genitals. Pyttalos remarked that an owl in town wouldn't know the Lady if it were to see her, and bore no significance whatever.

— They are religious about them at Athens, Lykas said. He was proud of his information, and looked at me with a congenial frankness, his head slightly lowered.

— The owl is Athene's sacred bird, I said.

— Owls, Pyttalos said, are the next thing to chickens.

— Who, I remarked as we reached the end of the street and had to wade through sheep being driven into town, are also sacred to Athene.

We came out onto a hill overlooking the river. Here we found the theater. It is quite old and charmingly small. The temple of Dionysos beside it was designed by Praxiteles. It, too, is small, but strong of line and brilliantly painted. Dionysos, the Eleans say, has never failed to attend their Thyia, the grounds for which are eight stadia from the town. Three empty jars are placed in the temple on the eve of the Elean Thyia, before any witnesses who care to watch, citizens or strangers. The doors are then sealed and guarded. Next morning, the seals are opened by the priests, and the jars are found to be filled with wine. The Andrioi have a similar visitation of the god. If one is to believe the Greeks about such things, one might as well believe the Aithiopians above Syene, who show a stone in a meadow which they call the table of the sun, where Helios dines. Religion is a grievous and wonderful thing.

Elis is as rich as Crete in vineyards. The god would certainly not be shy of showing himself to such diligent and worshipful votaries. The Thyia is a rite of deepest antiquity, the symbolism of which involves the winnowing basket, or *likna*, in which the infant Dionysos is said to have been cradled, the old reverence for bread and wine cherished by the Hellenes and indeed by the civilized world. The *likna* serves a third and purely religious function when it is filled by the priestesses with a toy of the god's phallos carved of fig wood. The harvest fruit is placed with it, awned wheat, gourds, leaves, and other bounty. This is then designated the cradle of Semele, and a hymn proclaims that the god is the son of his mother.

At Olympia we had seen the chair of Demeter Khamyne, whose lady bishop watches the contests, and Pyttalos explained that this Demeter is the same as Semele, or Zemele, as he called her.

— Mama of Zanysso, he added.

— She is, then, I said, the earth, and Dionysos is the vine.

— No, Kyrie, no, Pyttalos said. The earth is Zemele; the vine is Zanysso. But not all. The gods are more than we can know of them.

— We do not speak, O Kers!

— Touch wood, Pyttalos said.

As we walked back to our inn, all the asses of Elis began to bray, for it was their fodder time. Pyttalos and Lykas laughed, knowing my foreigner's opinion of this unnerving and peculiarly Aegean cacophony. If any other creature has the lungs of the Greek ass, I do not know it. I have heard the elephant trumpet, but its silver alarm has neither the volume nor the pitch of the Prienian ass, whose throat is of brass. And certainly none other of Zeus's animals has its satyric impudence, for like as not he accompanies his heart-stopping caterwaul with full priapic display of his considerable member, which leaps from its shaggy foreskin, for no other reason, I suppose, than that his daimon fulfills its being in his bray and pizzle, and that these proclaim their glory together, no doubt to the everlasting delight of the gods.

This incomparable voice is of composite majesty. In genus it is the whinny of the horse family, yet the lowing of cattle is folded in with the equine tune, and there is also to be detected in it the triumphant crow of the cock, the squealing of pigs, and the howling of dogs. And noises outside the cries of nature seem to figure in its awfulness, such as the stone saw, the whine of a gale in ships' rigging, the terrible lash of siege engines hurling missiles. Neither Pyttalos nor Lykas nor any Greek is disturbed by this piercing of the ear, a cry equally frantic whether in anticipation of supper, copulation, breakfast, or hoarfrost. Indeed, I suppose it is one of the strange Greek harmonies, an analogue of the aesthetic wherein the Hellenic adoration of the body is combined with the strictest and perhaps the purest of morals, and a fierce love of freedom exists within laws which a Tartar would deem tyrannical, and a sense of color rivaling that of the Egyptians expresses itself in coarse whites, drab terra cottas, and a single blue which one sees everywhere. Pyttalos never ceased to be all mirthful wrinkles when I winced at the *hgee! HGAH!* of the Greek ass, spilling my wine if I were raising it to my lips, or scoring my papyrus if I were making a note when one of these beasts called its god, its wife, or its master.

At the inn, waiting for supper, I stole the liberty of looking into the landlord's office. Whitewashed and splendidly provincial, it was hung with wineskins and strings of red onions, a sheepskin, baskets, fishing canes, straw hats, and, curious to note, a mask of some character in a play, a godly face with elegantly curled hair and beard. From the ceiling hung a cage of plaited grass in which the household's pet cricket sat folded up, waiting for the night.

We had goat for supper, with a soup of barley and scallions. Pyttalos found an herb in his wallet and broke it into his soup.

— For old age, he said, with a wink at Lykas.

I have sweetened my life with many far places, but I think none was more quietly congenial than the town of Elis. These were the streets which I now watched with their dogcarts in which matrons under parasols rode with the aplomb of Tanagra figurines, with their moustached promoters carrying game cocks under their arms, with their troops of brown athletes walking on the balls of their feet beside their trainers, superbly indifferent to the gaze of the girls' faces behind every curtain of beads, to the appraisal of the Spartan eye, and the higher appraisal of the Corinthian and Platonic stare, these were the streets that Pindaros had trod. Pythagoras had been here, and the philosophers Thales and Anaxagoras. Simonides, too. Even Diogenes, it is said. Hippias was born here.

We sat after dinner with our landlord Aristander and passed the evening with pleasantries. I asked if the tomb in the market which an old man had told me was that of Oxylos was not that of the ancient king of the Eleans.

— Who knows? he said. Is it not written somewhere?

— It is, I said, but one would expect a more prominent monument.

He expressed regret by opening and closing his hands, as if to apologize for the inexplicable remissness of the elders and archon of Elis.

— Probably too stingy to put up a proper stone, he said.

— Was he a god? Pyttalos asked.

— No, I said. Merely a king.

— As, Aristander said confidentially, were many of the gods that we now count among the immortals.

— So the philosophers say, I said, letting him know that I detected the source of his opinions.

— Graveyard talk, Pyttalos said. Because the gods have not come to their dreams or favored them with a *showing*—here he opened his ancient hands—they think there are no gods.

— I have heard the bull-roarer, Lykas ventured.

— My great aunt, Pyttalos went on, as if Lykas had not spoken, saw a centaur once. A philosopher came all the way from Epidauros to ask her about it. She was picking dandelions for a salad, a woman with no luck, born in a thunderstorm, and with a cast in her eye. Picking away, she was, and humming, most likely, as was her way, a hymn to the Lady, she was very religious, and looked up, and there in the broad daylight was the centaur. She bolted like the grandmother of all jack rabbits. She screamed all the way home. She went through briars and over walls, and looked as if she'd fought a lynx when she turned up in the yard, scaring everybody out of remembering their own names. For a week she kept to her bed, living off broth.

— To us she said it was wild and awful, *deinós*. When the philosopher came she said it was noble and religious. She cried as she told him about it, as if she'd seen the Lady or Maia.

I looked at my hands, my dusty feet.

— Did the centaur speak? Lykas asked.

— She didn't say, dear soul, Pyttalos sighed. She wouldn't have remembered a word if it had. Or would have added so much to what it said that the philosopher would have been there a week taking it down.

— Did she really see a centaur, Pyttalos? I asked.

— Who knows, he said. My grandfather saw Zeus.

Aristander looked into the wine jug.

— He was an eagle, Pyttalos continued. *He* spoke.

— An eagle talked! Lykas said.

— An eagle who was Zeus, I said gently.

Landlord Aristander pulled at the lobe of his ear and sat straighter.

We had to wait to hear was Zeus said while Pyttalos enjoyed his power to hold our attention. I passed him the wine bowl. He sipped and smoothed his whiskers.

— Grandfather Hippagoras, that was his name, was physicking the ass, sticking a turpentine and onion bolus down it. Cyrus was the ass's name, and there was considerable give and take in the business, as Pappa Hippagoras and Cyrus were both stubborn, and both famous for having their way. He had just got the bolus in and was on his knees holding the jaws of the ass closed with both arms, and it had just swallowed its medicine, with a kind of spasm in which, with a little more energy, it would have pulled its head off and jumped to Olympia, the eagle—Zeus—flew by and said, *Fine do!*

— Fine do! Lykas repeated.

Aristander seemed disappointed.

— He knows his animals, you see, Pyttalos explained.

We spent the evening talking of many things, the price of wool and wine, the games, the stars, the dilatoriness of the Roman bureaucracy, the wiles of tax collectors, until there were few people abroad in the streets, and Aristander was yawning politely behind his hand, Pyttalos openly, and Lykas had gone to sleep, his head on his shoulder.

Next day we said our farewells to Elis and set out on the road to Kyllene, the port of Elis on the Ionian. It has a good harbor, faces toward Sicily, and is a hundred and twenty stadia across the plain.

As we left the west gate, there ran by us a line of weary boys, jogging, naked, dull with dust. Their fatigue was evident in their ribs and eyes. They had run many a stadion, and breakfast was still before them. Had I been younger, I would have found great significance in their beauty, and shared their innocent knowledge of their own glory. But I took too much pleasure in the health of my middle years, thanks be to a generous fate and the kindly gods, to envy these striplings their brief splendor at the games, and found myself wishing for them the easy stamina to walk, when they are my age, across the world, and a soul to take it in.

The rich valley plains between Elis and Kyllene, now the color of stone in the late summer drought, bear the flax and hemp which the Eleans weave with every degree of fineness. Indeed, their linen is almost as fine as silk, which is not, as Pyttalos supposed, made from bark.

Silk, I explained, the manufacture of which is much misunderstood and practically a secret in the western world, is made by an insect from the land of the Seres; hence the Greek *ser*. This Serian insect, twice the size of our dung beetle, spins a web like the tree spider, which it also resembles in having eight feet. The Seres keep these insects in houses, safe from the weather, regulating the temperature for them according to the season. These creatures weave a fine thread, making a ball of it with their feet. For four years they are fed on millet, but in the fifth year, when their life span is almost over, they are fed with the tender leaves of the reed, their favorite food, which they eat until they burst, and more thread is found inside them. This is then woven into the finest of cloth.

When Pyttalos discovered that I had not been to the land of the Seres, he lost interest in my discourse.

Dust whitened us, got into our eyes and mouths, until we looked like millers. I reflected that men are what they eat, and that the Greek eats a lot of rock, and perhaps a lot of metal that is within rock, lime and iron. It is no wonder that the Greek picture of the world is wrought in rock and metal. He drinks rock in his mineral springs, breaths rock dust, and comes in time to look like rock, as Pyttalos does.

I shook dust in clouds from my tunic.

— We are approaching the sea, I said to Pyttalos, and one might reasonably expect to see a cloud or feel a breeze and, here I pointed to the bone-dry bed of a stream, perhaps rain. I was being city-bred and sardonic, and I detected the accusation in my idle re-mark that Pyttalos and his countrymen somehow loved, and even asked the gods, for an utter drought all summer long.

— Your swallow leaves in Metageitnion, he replied. After that we get new weather. The rain comes in Boedromion, and the wind. On the fourth day after the Scorpion rises, the Pleiades set at dawn. Then you get frost. The leaves are all down by then. My rheumatism goes into my fingers and knees. On the thirteenth, Lyra rises at dawn. Winter is here.

— And you sit by the fire eating roasted chickpeas, I said, and talk of the Medes and Persians.

He looked at me and sighed.

— I was quoting an old poem, I said.

We came to a field where women were winnowing beside a white house, their blue shirts stippled with chaff. Whether they were working or dancing was a pretty question, for they dipped the grain with their long baskets to a busy music which a bearded fellow played on the bouzouki, a peasant lyre with four sets of double strings. He could have been forty or a hundred years old. Greeks go from youth to old age with no apparent transition. He could have been Orpheus himself, older than the blue mountains beyond the fields. As we came abreast of them, we could make out the song.

> White was the moon
> And the stars in the river.
> O Anaktoria,
> Do you dream of Lysander?

> The dill was all yellow
> And gone was the clover,
> The mouse and the wheat-ear,
> The last of the summer.

To our surprise, Lykas began to sing in his high sweet voice, not yet that of a man.

> White was the robe
> She spread for her lover,
> White was the robe
> And embroidered the cover.

> But whiter by far
> Was the snow he lies under,
> And whiter the stars
> Where the hill foxes wander.

And then Pyttalos joined his grizzled voice, for the ballad was endless, and we walked on singing, toward Kyllene.

First there was the wrinkling glare of the sky to show us that we were not far from the coast, then that faint bitterness in our nostrils, the smell of all ports, and then, as we came to the top of a hill, the sea itself.

Below us lay Kyllene with her ships and warehouses, sunny streets and taverns.

Here, in some days, I was to sail to Italy. After dining on octopus, which the Kyllenians serve raw in a sauce of olive oil and herbs, we set out as diligently as ever to record the port's antiquities. There is a temple of Asklepios here, as well as a sanctuary to Aphrodita.

But the most imposing of their temples is to Hermes, protector of the city and its trade. The temple is old indeed, an archaic building with old-fashioned columns which would seem to owe their inspiration to the Phoenicians. Inside, upright on a round millstone, is a blackened shaft topped by what appeared at first to be a great acorn. Except for the dolmens of Sicily or perhaps the wild tall rocks of the Calabrian coast, I had never seen any stone so primeval in its import, nor so direct a symbol. It is, I should think, older than the idols of the Cyclades.

— But, I said, it is nothing more than a stone phallos.

— Yes, Pyttalos said, it is Hermes.

A Field of Snow
on a Slope of the Rosenberg

FOR A MAN who had seen a candle serenely burning inside a beaker filled with water, a fine spawn of bubbles streaming upward from its flame, who had been present in Zürich when Lenin with closed eyes and his thumbs hooked in the armholes of his waistcoat listened to the baritone Gusev singing on his knees Dargomyzhsky's *In Church We Were Not Wed*, who had conversed one melancholy afternoon with Manet's Olympia speaking from a cheap print I'd thumbtacked to the wall between a depraved adolescent girl by Egon Schiele and an oval mezzotint of Novalis, and who, as I had, Robert Walser of Biel in the canton of Bern, seen Professor William James talk so long with his necktie in his soup that it functioned as a wick to soak his collar red and caused a woman at the next table to press her knuckles into her cheeks and scream, a voyage in a hot-air balloon at the mercy of the winds from the lignite-rich hills of Saxony Anhalt to the desolate sands of the Baltic could precipitate no new shiver from my paraphenomenal and kithless epistemology except the vastation of brooding on the sweep of inconcinnity displayed below me like a map and perhaps acrophobia.

The balloon had shot aloft at Bittersfeld while with handsome Corsican flourishes and frisky rat-a-tat on the drum a silver cornet band diminishing below us to a spatter of brass and gold played *The Bear Went Over the Mountain*.

Cassirer lashed the anchor to the wicker taffrail and cried *auf Wiedersehen* to the shrinking figures below, ladies in leghorn bonnets, an engineer in a blue smock, an alderman waving his top hat, a Lutheran minister holding his bible like a brick that he had just been tossed, and little boys in caps and knee socks who envied our gauntlets, goggles, plaid mufflers, and telescope with fanatic eyes.

The winds into which we rose were as cold as mountain springs. Tattered wisps of clouds like frozen smoke hung around us. Unless you looked, you could not tell whether you sailed past the clouds or the clouds past you, and even then the Effect of Mach confused the eye, for the earth seemed to flow beneath the still gondola until this illusion could be dispelled, as when you look at a line drawing of a cube and sometimes see its far side as its front, Mach, who leaned over bridges and waited for the flip-flop of reality whereby he knew he was on a swift bridge flying down an immobile river, and none of us knows whether our train or the one beside us is sliding out of the station.

Cassirer turned and shook hands, gauntlet to gauntlet. I returned his toothy, Rooseveltian smile, though butterflies swarmed in my stomach, and a kitten tried to catch its tail.

Cassirer, able soul, adjusted blocks in tackle. Pink and violet clouds sank past us.

The balloon, O gorgeous memory, was as gaily painted as a Greek krater. An equatorial band paraded the signs of the zodiac around it. Red lozenges and green asterisks wreathed the top and neck. Ribbons streamed from the nacelle. The first ballast of sand was pouring down on the earth with the untroubled spill of an hourglass. Our shadow flowed over a red tile roof, a barn, three Holstein cows, a railroad track.

There was a dust of ice in the February wind into which we rose swinging like a pendulum.

When the perspective cube swaps its front plane for its back, have we not seen Einstein's *Relativitätstheorie* with our own eyes? Or do we see the cube this way with one skill of the brain and that way with another? The left of the brain, where intuitions leap like lightning, controls the dextrous right hand, logic, speech, our sense of space. The right of the brain, where reason stands alert, controls the awkward left hand, suspicion, primal fear, our sense of time.

— Thus, Cassirer continued with a shout, the animal man is a chiasmus of complementary and contradictory functions.

This conversation had been going on for days. People used to talk to each other, back then, as I now talk to myself. But you are there, *ich bitte tausendmal um Verzeihung!* Can you hear, in this wind, the F-dur *Erwachen heiterer Empfindungen bei der Ankunft auf den Lande?* I can. Cassirer kept up a conversation as it bobbed into his head, while descending from a train, at a urinal, in his hip bath, from outside my bedroom door in the middle of the night.

— Our minds combine the hysteria of a monkey, he said, with the level intellect of an English explorer.

I cupped my ear to hear in the emptiness of the wind.

— Irrational faith, he said while upending a sack of sand, holds faithless reason above the waves.

I looked down at the plats of fields, villages, and roads. I felt the weight of my body drain away. My fingers clutching the wicker of the gondola were as strengthless as worms.

— You are white, he shouted.

— Vertigo, I shouted back.

— Now you are green.

— *Das Schwindelgefühl!*

— Brandywine? he offered, handing me a chill flask.

Ach, das Jungsein! Now that I have passed through them, I know that there are no middle years. I have gone from adolescence to old age. There is a photograph of me as a goggled aeronaut. I looked like an acrobat from the *époque bleue et rose* of that charming rascal Picasso. If only *der Graf* Rufzeichen could have seen me then! It would have been a shock worth arranging to confront the *adlig* old horse's behind with his melancholy butler at such an altitude.

Lisa would have screamed, and Herr Benjamenta of the Institute would have frowned his frown, rumpling the wrinkles of a vegetable marrow into his pedagogical brow.

Knolls, canals, fields, farms, slid below us. We were like Zeus in the *Ilias* when he surveys the earth from the mare's milk drinkers beyond the Oxus to the convivial herdsmen of Ethiopia.

— Altdorfer! Cassirer shouted. Dürer! Is this not, *mein geliebt*

Walser, the view of beroofed and steepled Northern Europe you
see from Brueghel's Tower of Babel? The splendor of it! Look at
that haystack, that windmill, that Schloss. You can see greenhouses.
Have you ever been taken so by the paralleleity of light?

We saw red and gold circus wagons on the turnpike, followed
by elephants, each holding the tail of the next with its trunk.

Did Nietzsche go up in a balloon? After Nietzsche, as the wag
said, there had to be Walser. Did Buonaparte? I tried to feel like
each in turn, to lounge like Nietzsche, blind and postured, with
some lines of Empedokles for Fräulein Lou, to pout my corpora-
tion like the *Empereur*, pocket my fingers in my weskit, and think
Caesar.

But, *O Himmel*, it was Count Rufzeichen I wanted as a ravaged
and outraged witness to my *Ballonfahrt*. It was as an orphan under
his roof that I came nearest to belonging anywhere at all, except
here, perhaps. Perhaps.

I arrived at his estate sneezing and ruffled a wild blustery day
that had reddened my ears and rolled my stovepipe hat before
me. Why Benjamenta had specified a stovepipe hat for going off
to one's first position will be known only at the opening of the
seals. To catch my hat I abandoned my cardboard suitcase to the
mercy of the rain, which went for its seams. In the hat was my di-
ploma, signed and sealed, from Herr Benjamenta's Institute for
Butlers, Footmen, and Gentlemen's Gentlemen. My umbrella was
the sort *Droschkenkutscher* saw their fares safely to shelter with,
copious enough to keep dry a lady in bombazeen, bustle, and
extensive fichu even if she were escorted by an *ukrainischer
Befehlshaber* in court dress. The wind played kite with it.

My hat had hopped, leaving rings of its blacking on the gleaming wet of the flagstones. My umbrella tugged and swiveled,
jerked and pushed. I ran one way for the suitcase, another for the
stovepipe hat. Were anyone looking from the stately mansion, it
was the grandfather of all umbrellas on two legs tiptoeing like a
gryllus after a skating hat across a sheet of shining water they
would see.

The cook Claribel had seen, and would allude to it thereafter
as a sight that gave her pause.

Unsettled as my affiliation with the morose Count Rufzeichen
had been, it was a masonic sodality compared with my and Clari-

bel's crosscurrent encounters. Our disasters had been born in the stars.

It was she who met me at the door, challenge and hoot in her hen's eyes.

— Is this, I shouted over the wind, Schloss Dambrau?

To this she made no reply.

— I am Monsieur Robert, I said, the new butler.

She studied me and the weather, trying to decide which was the greater affront to remark upon.

— As you can see, she finally said, there is no butler here to answer the door. A cook, the which I am, can make her own meals, but a butler, like the new one you are, *ja?* cannot answer himself knocking at the door, *fast nie.*

I agreed to all of this.

— Would you guess I am Silesian? she next offered. Frau Claribel you may address me as. Why the last butler had to leave is not for one of my sex and respectability to say, I'm sure. What were you doing running in a crouch all over the drive? Furl your umbrella. Come in out of the wind, come in out of the rain.

I marched to my quarters, past a cast-iron Siegfried in the foyer, preceded by Frau Claribel with the mounted, cockaded Hessians, royal drum rolls, and jouncing flag of Haydn's *Symphonie militaire,* which came all adenoidal violins and tinny brass from a gramophone beyond a wall.

— *Der Graf* is very cultivated, she said of the music. He has tone, as you will see, Herr *Robehr.*

I approved of the Lakedaimonian bed in my room. And of the antique table where I was to spend so many hours by my candle, warming my stiff hands at a brazier. All my rooms have been like this, cramped cells for saint or criminal. Or patient. The chamberpot was decorated with a sepia and pink view of Vesuvius.

O Claribel, Claribel. No memory of her can elude for long our first *contretemps.* That is too bookish a word. Our wreck.

It was only the third day after my installment, just when the Count and I were blocking out the routine that would lead, from the very beginning, to my eventual banishment to a room above the Temperance Society of Biel for eight years, while archdukes died with bombs in their laps, ten million men were slaughtered, six million maimed, and all the money in the world five times over was borrowed at compound interest from banks. Solemn, hushed, sacred banks.

On my way in haste down the carpeted hall to answer the Count's bell, I would prance into a cakewalk, strutting with backward tail feather and forward toe. I would hunch my elbows into my side, as if to the sass of a cornet in a jazz band I would tip a straw hat to the house. And just before the library door I would do the war dance of Crazy Horse. Then, with a shudder to transform myself into a graduate of the Benjamenta Institute, I would turn the knob with one hand, smooth my hair with the other, and enter a supercilious butler deferential and cool.

— You rang, Herr Graf?

The old geezer would have to swivel around in his chair, an effect I could get by pausing at the periphery of his vision, a nice adjustment between being wholly out of sight and the full view of an indecorous frontal address.

— I rang, by Jove, didn't I? I wonder why.

— I could not say, Sir.

— Strange.

— You rang, Sir, unless by some inadvertence your hand jerked the bell cord, either out of force of habit, or prematurely, before the desire that would have prompted the call had formed itself coherently in your mind.

Count Rufzeichen thought this over.

— You heard the bell, did you, there in the recess?

— Positively, Sir.

— Didn't imagine it, I suppose, what?

— No, Sir.

— I'm damned, the Count said, gazing at his feet. Go away and let me think why I called you.

— If, Sir, you would jot down on a pad the reason for my summons, you would not forget it before my arrival.

— Get out!

— Very good, Sir.

We played such scenes throughout the day. I had just had some such mumpery with him before the first entanglement with Claribel's withered luck.

She, barefoot for scrubbing the stone steps down to her domain, had forked a lid off the stove onto the floor to pop on a stick of firewood, and as the best piece in the box was longish, Claribel stepped back the better to fit it in, putting a foot both naked and wet on the hot lid, and cried out for Jesus to damn it for a bugger and a shit britches.

I, meanwhile, coming belowstairs and hastening to see what her howl was about, stepped on the cake of soap riding there on the steps in a wash of suds. My foot slid out and up in a kick so thorough that I missed by a minim marking the ceiling with a soapy footprint.

My other foot, dancing for balance, dashed the bucket of water forward toward the hopping Claribel, where its long spill hissed when it flowed around the lid at about the same time that I, soaring as if from a catapult, rammed her in a collision that knocked us breathless and upside-down through the kitchen door and into a dogcart drawn by a goat which was backed up to the steps for a convenient unloading of cowflop to mulch the rhododendrons.

Startled, the goat bleated and bolted, taking us through the kitchen garden, across the drive, into and out of the roses, around the well, by the stables, and as far as the chicken run, where a yellow wheel, unused to such velocities and textures of terrain, parted from the axle and went on its own to roll past backing pigs, a cat who mounted a tree at its coming, a cow who swallowed her cud, and after some delirious circles, wobbled and lay among the wasps and winey apples in the orchard.

Claribel and I, tilted out by the departure of the wheel, sat leg over leg in the compost of manure, Claribel screaming, I silent.

THIS WAY. The bracken is very fine a little farther on. Trajectory is all. I was born on Leonardo da Vinci's birthday the year the bicycle suddenly became popular all over the world, the seventh of eight. My father ran a toy shop in which you could also buy hair oil, boot blacking, and china eggs. My mother died when I was sixteen, after two years of believing that she was a porcupine that had been crowned the queen of Bulgaria, the first sign that I was to end up here.

My brother Ernst, grown enough to be teaching school while I was still in rompers, began to think that he was being hunted by malevolent marksmen. Schizophrenia. He died in 1916, Hermann, a geographer in Bern, in 1919. Fanny and Lisa are well placed, Oskar works with money. Karl is the success in the family. God knows how he can stomach Berlin.

I was at Waldau before I came here, into the silence. And before that—look at the rabbit standing on its hind legs!—I was variously a student, a bank clerk, an actor, a poet, a sign painter, a soldier—I have seen those white butterflies as thick as snow over clover—an insurance salesman, a waiter, a vendor of puppets, a bill sticker, a janitor, a traveling salesman for a manufacturer of prosthetic limbs, a novelist, a butler, an archivist for the canton of Bern, and a distributor of temperance tracts. I've always belonged decidedly to the tribe of Whittington, but of course the bells rang when I couldn't hear them, and when a cat was to be invested I had none. Franklin was of the tribe, and Lipton the British merchant, and Mungo Park, and Lincoln and Shakespeare. I got as far as being a servant. Diogenes and Aesop were slaves.

Freedom is a choice of prisons. One life, one death. We are an animal that has been told too much, we could have done with far less. The way up and the way down are indeed the same, and Heraklit had been wiser to add that rising is an upward fall.

I often put myself to sleep by wondering if there could be a mountain road so steep and yet so zigzag of surface that in seeming to go down an incline one is actually going up?

How do *they* put themselves to sleep, Mann of the field marshal's face and Hesse with his gurus and Himalayan Sunday Schools? Imagine being interested like Hesse in the Hindu mind! Once in Berlin I talked to an Indian from Calcutta or Poona or Cooch. *Chitter chitter*, he said. Mann is also interested in these little brown monkey men with women's hands.

— What is the meaning of life? the little Hindu asked me for an opener.

I had the distinct impression that he was switching his tail and flouncing his cheek ruff. Soon he would be searching for lice in my hair.

— You do not know! In the west you are materialistic, rational, scientific. You listen too much to the mind, too little to the soul. You are children in spirit. You have not *karma*.

We stood nose to nose, toe to toe.

— You have not deep wisdom from meditation a long time reaching back to ages already old when Pletto and Aristettle were babbies in arms.

— Indeed not, I said.

— You admit! the Hindu squealed, showing a gold tooth and a black. Of course you admit for you know it is true ancient Indian wisdom is universal transcendental thought as studied by Toolstoy in Russia, yes, H. B. Stove and Thorough in United States.

He chittered on, something about God and man being like a mother cat with a kitten in her teeth and man and God being like a monkey and its infant holding on, and something about emptying the mind when what I wanted to empty was my bladder.

O glide of eye and sizzle of tongue! And Rathenau found me a job in German Samoa. And he was shot, like a mad dog, because, as his assassin Oberleutnant Kern explained, *he was the finest man of our age, combining all that is most valuable of thought, honor, and spirit, and I couldn't bear it.* I told this to the doctor here, in an unguarded moment, and he asked me why I was obsessed by such violence. Cruelty, I replied, is sentimentality carried to its logical conclusion.

— Ah! he said.

The psychiatric *ah.*

— We can never talk, I said, for all my ideas are symptoms for you to diagnose. Your science is suspicion dressed in a tacky dignity.

— Herr Walser, Herr Walser! You promised me you would not be hostile.

They are interested in nothing, these doctors. They walk in their sleep, looking with the curiosity of cows at those of us who are awake even in our dreams.

A moth slept flat on my wall. I watched its feelers, speckled feathers as remote from my world as I from the stars, sheepsilver wings eyed with apricot and flecked with tin. It had dashed at the bulb of my lamp. Its fury was like a banker's after money. And now it was weary and utterly still. Did it dream? The Englander Haldane had written of its enzymes without killing a single moth, and wore bedbugs in a celluloid pod on his leg to drink his blood.

It is in Das Evangelium the brother of rust and thieves. Surely its sleep is like that of fish, an alert sloth.

Now it has fluttered onto the map above my desk, an old woodcut map from a book, the river Euphrates running up through it in a dark fullness of rich veins, the Garden of Eden below, the stout mountains of Armenia sprinkled along the top, a great tower and swallow-tailed pennon to mark Babylon, trees as formal as pine cones at the terrestrial paradise, with Adam and Eve as naked as light bulbs except for Akkadian skirts of tobacco sheaves, Greek and Hebrew names among Latin like flowers among leaves, a lion to the northwest sitting in Armenia and bigger than a mountain, a beast rich in horns and hair stepping west from the Caspian Sea, a route pompous with Alexander's cities, brick walls and fig groves of Scripture, Caiphat up from the Gulf of Persia, which Sindbad gazed upon and where bdellium is to be had, Bahrim Insula a pearl fishery, Eden with its four rivers green and as straight as canals, a grove of cypress that was felled to build the Ark, purple Mousal, Babylon a city of brick and a hundred temples to gods with wings like aeroplanes, with Picassoid eyes and Leonardonian beards, Ur of the Chaldees with its porched and gabled house of Abraham, Noah's city Chome Thamanon, Omar's Island, with mosque, the Naarda of Ptolemy where is a famous school of the Jews, Ararat's cone, Colchis with its fleece of gold, Phasis the country of pheasants, Cappadocia, Assyria, Damascus under an umbrella of date palms.

And then I saw that the moth was inside the light bulb.

BECAUSE, I said when asked why I am here, the world was in defiance of its own laws.

At the foot of Herr Rufziechen's grand stairs stood a cast-iron Siegfried braced with a boar-sticker and buckler outsinging a surge of Wagnerian wind that tilted his horns, butted his beard, and froze his knees. Did he have to be dusted? Thoroughly, thoroughly. Beyond him, in steep gloom, rose the stairs in a curve of crimson and oak.

On a stepladder, flipping the face of iron Siegfried with a turkey duster, I, remembering that if you stare through a window into a snowfall the room will rise and the snow stand still, as when down front close to a theater curtain, the audience sinks grandly, to trumpets, discovering below a red Tannhäuser kneeling beside an embroidered Venus singing *Zu viel, Zu viel, O dass ich nun erwachte!* saw Count Rufzeichen gliding from the library with his nose in a book and Claribel the cook backing toward him, the mock orange in her arms. The precision with which they would collide was inevitable and perverse.

— *Zu viel!* I cried.

Rammed from behind, Claribel screamed, heaved the mock orange upward, and sat.

I tottered, embraced Siegfried, and lost the ladder under my dancing toes.

The mock orange fell upside down on Count Rufzeichen, filling his lap with earth and roots. It was as if an allegory of Horticulture, with Donor, had fallen out of a picture onto the museum floor.

The ladder completed its fall across Rufzeichen's shins, inciting him into a jumping-jack flip over Claribel, transferring the mock orange's empty bucket from his head to hers, which made her screams now sound hollow, as if from the depths of a well.

GLIDING OVER the firelit carpet with velvet steps, placing the tureen before my lord, who touches his napkin to his moustache, I can savor again the condition of my well-being, along with the aroma of leek and broth that steams up when I remove the lid with a gesture worthy of the dancers of Bali, namely that Rufzeichen has put me back together, suave foot, accurate hand, impeccable diction.

Genius is time.

There was, I knew, and remembered with fondness, a professor at the Sorbonne who electrocuted himself while lecturing, or electrocuted himself so nearly that he found that he was suddenly in a corner just under the ceiling, light as a Chagall bridegroom full of champagne. And yet he could see himself still lecturing below, calmly, giving no indication that an ox's weight of lightning had crashed through his body.

Then he realized that his feet, shod and gaitered, were on opposite sills. His torso was in orbit around the lamp. His left arm was in the cloakroom nervously fingering a galosh, his right caressed a periodic table of the elements. His rich, musically modulated voice lectured on about ohms and circuits, resistance and watts.

It was my own parable. I had searched for wisdom about the slump of my soul and the sootiness of my spirit in the accounts of vastations by the American Jameses, father and son, who suffered terrible New England moments when all significance drained from the world, when the immediate fortune of life was despair, disease, death. In utter futility shone the sun, man squandered the little time he had alive, a sweet Tuesday here, a golden autumn Sunday there, grubbing for money to pay the butcher, the land-lord, and the tailor. The butcher slaughtered innocent animals who were incapable of sin and folly, of ambition or lies, so that one could, by way of a cook enslaved for a pittance and a wife enslaved for naught, gnaw its flesh and after a period of indigestion and indolence from overfeeding, squat over a champerpot and drop turds and piss for a servant to carry, holding his nose, to the lime pit.

I had thought my despair was Kierkegaard's sickness unto death that pleasure cloys and pain corrodes. But, no, it was rather the Sorbonne professor's shock. One came to pieces. One used the very words. You had to pull yourself together again.

Feeding the pages of three novels into the fire in Berlin, stand-ing in the rain at my father's grave, writing my thousandth *feuilleton,* climbing the dark stairs to any of the forty rooms I've rented: no one movement of foot or heart muscle was the hobbler, no one man's evasion the estranger.

— Another pig's foot, your lordship?

— And a little more suet, thank you kindly, Robert.

White tile, thermometers, blood-pressure charts, urine speci-mens, and spasms in the radiator pipes; what color and tone there had been at Rufzeichen's! The carpet, a late Jugendstil pattern of compact circles in lenticular overply, rusty orange, Austrian brown, and the blue of Wermacht lapels, had dash, and the furni-ture was Mackintosh, smartly modern in its severity while recall-ing the heaviest tradition of knightly chairs and ladylike settles, sideboards as large as wains and a desk at which the Kaiser could plan a dress parade. My eye appreciated the dull books around him, china shepherdesses, views of Florence and Rome, a sepia reproduction of the Sistine Chapel ceiling, crossed cavalry sabers, a teakwood dragon in a rage, candlesticks held aloft by fat babies tiptoe on the noses of dolphins, a loud clock.

An iron elk stood in a dim recess beyond double doors in the far wall.

AND THEN, pigeon-toed and watching the ground before him as if backtracking for something lost, there was the new patient, Fomich, as his wife or sister called him. The first time I saw him I did not like his silly smile. The mad smile in their own way, as puppets step, with a jerk rather than civilized deliberation. The smile of Fomich was that of the imp, of the red goblin in the corner of Füssli's *Titania und Bottom*. Smirk and scowl together it was.

It was the outward concession of inner reserve, two proud men meeting, each believing the other to be of higher rank.

— *Kak tsiganye!* he complained to his sister or wife.

And then I saw the muscles bunched in his shoulders that had strained the threads of the armscye apart, the heft of his chest, the improbable narrowness of his hips. Hero, with wing, grounded.

They took a walk together every morning and afternoon, solicitous woman and elfin man. Sometimes he would stop, put his heels together, flex his knees, and pass his hands in a sweep from one hip to the other.

One day, to my disbelieving gaze, he jumped over a rose bush without so much as a running start. Faces appeared at windows to watch.

He jumped back over the rose bush, his eyes sleepy and sad.

IT WAS LIKE striding over a sea of gelatin, that bell-stroke swing of our nacelle through the rack of the upper air on elastic wicker, wind thrumming the frapping with the elation of Schumann strings *allegro molto vivace*.

We talked by cupping hands and shouting into each other's

ears. Benjamin Franklin, Cassirer said, had wanted a balloon for moving about the streets of Philadelphia, rooftop high above the Quakers and Indians. He was to have hitched it to horses, a god-like man indeed.

— Ach, les Montgolfier, Joseph and Etienne! In those days they thought smoke was a gas, as right as they were wrong, as with all knowledge. A transparent blue October day they bundled the physicist Pilâtre de Rozier into the basket of their hot-air balloon and cheered him aloft over the Bois de Boulogne. There, anchored twenty-five meters above the Jardin de la Muette, he looked down on autumn and Lilliputians flapping handkerchiefs. He fed the stove that kept him up there a truss of straw, scanned the horizon with a telescope, took a barometric reading.

— The next month he and the Marquis d'Arlandes went up without a tether, floated across Paris for half an hour, and came down at La Butte-aux-Cailles, where wind had carried them. Peasants were waiting to kill the balloon with scythes and shovels.

History is a dream that strays into innocent sleep.

And everything is an incongruity if you study it well. When, wind plucking my nose and fetching the moment back, I was sent on an errand one day by Herr Benjamenta to buy pen nibs from the stationer and three pounds of Brussels sprouts from the greengrocer, the latter to energize us for writing a round and legible hand with the former, the morning being summery and fine, what should I see straightway, so wonderful is the world, but the handle of a sweep's broom tipping the hat of a stout and grizzly old party into the bucket of a passing house painter, where it bobbed and lolled in a creamy distemper, while, as if miracles hadn't grown scarce in our time, a grackle with determined eye swooped down and snatched off the same old party's curly red wig, taking it over a roof before the street could frame a single sentence of articulate consternation.

— His hat is in the bucket, a little girl said to her nurse.

— Yes, said the nurse, there it goes.

— That grackle, said a bearded gentleman, took off his wig.

The nurse acknowledged the gentleman's remark by blushing. The little girl did him a curtsy. I stood as in a dream.

The old party, meanwhile, stopped dumbfounded, his hands

to his naked head, where a fringe of reddish hair enwreathed his occipital salience. It pleased me that he had not chosen so red a wig without cause.

— The man is distracted, explained the nurse to her charge. See how he rolls his eyes and chews his moustache.

— Yes, said the little girl. This is something I can tell to Ermintrude. She will be beside herself with jealousy.

Whereupon, weeping with such feeling that both cheeks shone like glass, the old party hugged himself so furiously that his coat split down the back. The sound of this was that of a dry limb cracked by wind from a tree, and he went limber as if unstrung.

The left half of his coat slid, sleeve and all, onto the sidewalk, followed by the right half, sleeve and all.

The collar, I considered, drawing closer, should have held the two halves together, but no, upon inspection, I saw that it was a coat, Moravian or Sephardic, of the kind that has no collar.

A scarf, which even now, as the old party was running back and forth imploring God and the gendarmerie to witness that he was a victim of some untoward fracture of natural law, snagged on the spike of an area railing and whipped away with an elastic flounce, never to be seen on this earth by its owner again.

The waywardness of accidents, I mused, can go only so far until it collides with the laws of probability or the collapse of its martyr.

The old party sat down on the sidewalk and wept into his hands. The gentleman with the beard came to his aid, prefacing his remarks by saying kindly that he had seen all that had happened. Here the old party gasped, alluded to his heart, and fell backward.

— I do believe, said the nurse, that he is having some sort of fit.

— *Zu hilfe! Zu hilfe!* cried the bearded gentleman.

— I will do an imitation of this, said the little girl, rolling back her eyes and grabbing her throat, that will make Ermintrude hate herself for a week.

— Remember that you are in public, said the nurse.

— So is he, said the little girl.

— And it is ill-bred in both of you, said the nurse, to make a spectacle on a city street.

A crowd gathered, from which a slender man in dark glasses, explaining that his uncle was a pharmacist in Lichtenstein, ad-

vised that the old party's waistcoat be undone. Deftly the gentleman undid fourteen buttons, disclosing trousers that came up to
the armpits in the manner of the English. The flies of these were
undone as far as the navel, fourteen more buttons, and indeed
the old party groaned and breathed more freely, it seemed.

— *Polizei!* screamed the nurse.

The laces of his boots should be untied, the Lichtenstein pharmacist's nephew said, and the suspenders of his stockings loosened,
for circulation's sake.

— I will, said the bearded gentleman, take his watch, wallet,
tie pin, and ring for safekeeping, lest they tempt someone here
in the crowd.

— My watch! squealed the old party, kicking with such indignation that both boots leapt off his feet. A dog got one and made
off with the agility of a weasel. The other bounced into the gutter,
where it lay forlorn and strange in the brief moment before a
policeman arriving on the trot shot it along the curbing to drop
into a drain. We could all hear it bumping on its way through
gurgling water to the river Aar.

— Let us see if his name is written inside his shirt, said the
policeman, lifting the old party by the armpits and taking off
his waistcoat.

— What is this? he exclaimed, peeling a mustard plaster from
the old party's back.

— That, said the pharmacist's nephew, is probably the cause
of his fit. It is a poultice of asafoetida, mustard, and kerosene
such as country doctors prescribe for pulmonary and liver com-
plaints. It is too strong, as you can smell, and has induced an
apoplexy. Take off his shirt and undervest to air his back.

Struggling to arrange the old party, the bearded gentleman
inadvertently stood on both his loose stocking suspenders, anch-
oring them, so that as the body was dragged backward the better
to extract the long shirt tail from inside the seat of the trousers,
the elastic suspenders stretched their limit, snapped, flipped, and
catapulted themselves and stockings together off the old party's
feet, one flying into my face. And, O, how I was gratified to have
joined the event with something of my own, and I sneezed, casting stocking and suspender into the shopping basket of a cook
who, later and at home, dropped them into her stove, making a

hex. The other was got from the air by a dog who had envied his fellow the previous shoe.

At this moment, crazed with fury and mindless with disbelief, the old party fought his way up to choke the policeman, losing trousers and drawers as he stood.

— Attack the law, will you! the policeman said.

— Where am I? the old party cried. *Who* am I? What has happened?

He was as naked as the minute he was born, minus, of course, an umbilical cord.

— *Scheisse und verdammt!* It comes back to me that I am Brigadegeneral Schmalbeet. That's who I am! General Schmalbeet!

With this he gave the policeman a kick in the groin that doubled him over.

Then he fell backward, an arc of urine following him down. Everyone backed away. When I peeped around the first corner I had turned, I saw the policeman wetting a pencil with his tongue while opening a notebook, and a dog dragging away the old party's trousers, and another throwing his drawers into the air and barking.

MANET'S OLYMPIA, thumbtacked to the wall between a depraved adolescent girl by Egon Schiele and an oval mezzotint of Novalis, told me about the world's first painting executed *en plein air*. This was the work of her creator's *Doppelgänger* Monet, Manet with an *omega*.

— I am confused already, said I. But talk on, for it adds purpose to my staring at you, at your complacent Parisian eyes, your dangling mule, your hand so decorously audacious.

— *Êtes-vous phallocrate?*

— *L'homme est un miroir omnigénérique, tantôt plan, tantôt convexe, tantôt concave ou cylindrique, donnant à l'objet réfléchi des dimensions variées.*

— *Vous êtes phallocrate.*

— *Suis-je donc?*

— *Ce ne fait rien.*

Her Ionic shoulders rose an ironic trifle. There was the wisp of a smile in the corners of her mouth, the merest hint of laughter in her eyes.

— When, she said, in the pellucid green air of Fontainebleau, Claude Monet had posed his model and touched his brush to the world's first *plein air* canvas, he was hit on the back of the head by a discus and knocked senseless.

Her expression did not change as she made this statement.

— A discus?

— *Un disque.*

— The discobolus, she continued, who presently appeared on the anxious trot to ask the bloody impressionist and the screaming Madame Monet if they had seen his quoit was a bassetted and spatted Englishman whose carp's mouth and plaid knickerbockers sprang from the pages of Jerome K. Jerome.

Count Rufzeichen, anglophile and sportsman, dressed so. It was his sedulous imitation of the English that had driven him to hire a butler, and thus I came to tread his soft carpets, never tiring of their luxurious silence, or of the rose fragrance of English tea, or of making Herr Rufzeichen shake his wattles.

One way was to be deaf to his summons, letting the butler's bell jangle in vain. After awhile, the old apteryx would come puffing and snuffling along, looking into rooms. Finding me in the greenhouse, he would splay his fingers and shout.

— What in the name of God are you doing?

— Sir, I am observing nature, I would reply. I see, however, that in lending my attention to the limpidity of the air, the melodiousness of the cuckoo and the lowing of the horned cattle I have fallen into negligence.

— Into sloth, said Herr Rufzeichen.

— The cows made a kind of bass for the treble of the cuckoo.

— Into impudence.

— Your worship rang?

— To little purpose, to no purpose, Monsieur Robert. Whatever I wanted you for before, it's a liver attack I'm having at the moment.

The Count trembled into a chair.

— Would you wish a glass of Perrier, Sir?

— *Doppelkohlensaures Natron.*

The Count pulled a pocket handkerchief big as a map of

Europe from his sleeve, wadded it with both hands, and wiped away the sweat that had beaded on his forehead.

I held the soda on a silver salver under his nose. The draught drunk, hiccups set in. After the third hiccup, a belch baritone and froggy.

Outside the asylum gates a brass band huffed and thumped with brazen sneezes, silver whiffets, thundering sonorities and a detonating drum, the descant hitched together by a fat woman in a Tyrolese hat and the Erlkönig's longcoat that flocked upon her hips as she squeezed and pulled a Polish accordion as big as a sheep, dipping her knees on the *saltarelli* and rolling her eyes in a clown's gloat.

The man Fomich danced around his pleased sister, seesawing his shoulders in a backward monkeyshine of steps, and as he shot into the air right over his sister's head, pausing there awhile as if all the clocks in the world had stopped, a lunatic shouted that Hitler is the seventh disaster in Nostradamus and invited all within hearing to join the Brotherhood of the Illuminati without further delay.

— Quite gay, is it not? I said to the attendant, tears in my eyes.

The band was charging with piston gallop through something rhapsodic, Hungarian, and tacky.

Who was this franion? There was a *grivoiserie* about him that smacked of Berlin, and of things brooded on in Mallarmé, Rimbaud, Apollinaire.

— Literature, I said to the listless woman beside me on the bench, has become a branch of psychology, of politics, of power, of persuasion, of housekeeping. In ancient times . . .

— When Jesu was a little boy, she said, taking interest and joining her hands on her knees.

— In ancient times literature was a story for people to hear. And the person who heard it could tell it to another. Now everything is on paper, too complex to remember.

— Do you love Jesu? she asked.

— One does not write in this terrible age. We do not make chairs, we make money. We do not make shoes, we make money. They sniff it, banker and shopkeeper alike, as gallants used to inhale the perfume of a mistress's handkerchief. They goggle when they see it, they are willing and eager to throw boys into the spew of machine guns and fogs of cyanide gas, they are abustle to marry their daughters to toothless bankers, to halitosic financiers with hernias the size of a baby's head. Francs, yen, shillings, pesos, krönen, dollars, lire, money is the beauty of the world. They suck shekels and play with themselves.

— Jesu would not like that, she said mournfully.

— After all, I said, what a beautiful thing it is, not to be, but to have been a genius.

The dancer had collapsed across the way, was weeping and was being consoled by his sister.

— Does God come to you in the night, she asked, with a lamp and a puppy for you to hold?

— God, I said, is the opposite of Rodin.

— The eyes of God are as beautiful as a cow's.

— Everything else has gone wrong, but not money. Everything, everything is spoiled, halved, rotted, robbed of grace and splendor. Our cities are vanishing from the face of the earth. Big chunks of nothing are taking up the space once occupied by houses and palaces.

— You are very serious, she said.

— Money precludes mercy.

— Did you have money and lose it? Jesu would not mind that.

— I have always been poorer than the poor.

Attendants had come to take the man Fomich back to his cell. He was saying terrible things about man's sexuality, so that the woman beside me stopped her ears. I could hear something about the hot haunches of goats and wild girls in Arcadia kissing something and something mad with music.

If I could talk again with Olympia, she would tell me. She would know.

Is IT NOT preposterous that a shoe would go the journey of a foot?

AND ON A fine English day in the high Victorian year 1868, the year of the first bicycle race and the Trades Union Congress at

Manchester, of *The Moonstone* and *The Ring and the Book* and
of the siege of Magdala, four men gathered at Ashley House in
London, a house leafy with Virginia creeper, its interior har-
moniously dark and bright, like an English forest, dark with
corners and doors and halls, with mahogany and teak and drapes
as red as cherries, bright with windows, Indian brass, and lamps
like moons, Lord Lindsay pollskepped with the hatchels of a
cassowary, Lord Adare whose face looked like a silver teapot, and
the galliard Captain Wynne.

They stood Englishly around a bandy-legged Scot with a
thrummy beard. His name was Home. Daniel Douglas Home.

— Tack a wheen heed, he said, throwing back his neck and arms
as if throttled by an angel from above.

In contempt of gravity, then, he raised his left leg and his right,
and lay out flat on the empty air.

— Stap my vitals! swore Captain Wynne. The bugger's floating!

Lord Lindsay held up Lord Adare, Lord Adare Lord Lindsay.

— Meet me, gasped the horizontal Scot, in the tither room.

With a hunch to get started, he slid forward before their par-
alyzed gaze, jerking a whit on the first slide, and then floated
smoothly, silently out the window.

A distant chime of church bells: which no one heard.

— I think I shall cat, said Lord Lindsay.

— I have peed myself, said Lord Adare.

The feet of D. D. Home appeared in the next window: he had
turned right. His sturdy Glaswegian trousers next, his plaid waistcoat, his arms hanging down slightly, fingers spread, his heroic
Adam's apple, eyes staring upward.

His shadow three stories below flowed over rose bushes, over
rolled grass as level as water, a sundial, the body of a gardener
who had looked up, commended his soul to God, and passed out.

Lords and captain bestirred themselves, dashed into each other,
and ran down the hall on uncooperative legs. Only the door to
a room on the other side of the house was open, and into this they
stumbled, breathing like rabbits. Adare screamed as he saw Home
entering the window feet first, calm as a corpse.

Midroom he hung in the air, chuckling.

Then he tilted downward and stood as proud as Punch.

— Bewitched, by the Lord! said Captain Wynne. We are all bewitched.

Lord Lindsay's hair had turned white.

Yet all three signed depositions that they had witnessed a human Scot float out the window of Ashley House and in again from the other side.

Home died soon after.

— And now, I said to Herr Rufzeichen, how shall we ever know otherwise?

— Englishmen, said Rufzeichen, of all people! Sort of thing that goes on every day in India, I believe?

AT THE BENJAMENTA INSTITUTE I was like a cuckoo in a nest of wrens. I had failed at just about everything and the other students of the art of butlering had failed only predestination, and even that wasn't certain, for we were told daily that Joseph was a butler in Egypt and Daniel one in Babylon. Their slain and risen god was Dick Whittington. The rotten stockings they darned in the evenings were Whittington's, their cold beds were Whittington's, their slivers of soap, their piecemeal and unmatching shoe laces, their red ears and round shoulders.

A feature of failure is having to do over again what the successful sailed through once. My adolescence has been waiting for me when my feet hit the floor every morning these seventy years. My God, what a prospect! An education, a job, a wife, daughters to admire, sons to counsel, vacations at Ostend, retirement, grandchildren, banquets in my honor, statesmen and a mountain of flowers at my funeral, my sepulcher listed in the tourist guide to the cemetery.

And in middle age I was enrolled in a school for butlers.

The dormitory was upstairs, a long room with too many beds too close together. It was neither military in its effect nor schoolish, neither neat nor messy. It was a picture of despair and of making do.

I remember it all as a dream in which confusion had seeped into the grain of reality. I remember yellow-haired Hans, and defeated Töffel, of the bitten fingernails and wetted bed, the clever Kraus and his intolerable and boring cynicism, the flippant and windy Fuchs who cried under the covers at night. We all led secret lives in full view of each other.

Herr and Frau Benjamenta, accomplished frauds, came and went like attendants in a hospital. All day we heard homilies and half-finished sentences from retired Gymnasium teachers and had lessons in ironing trousers and setting tables. We heard Scripture at dawn and before bedtime. Of all this I made my novel *Jakob von Gunten*, a new kind of book, and except for a few of the essays I wrote for newspapers, essays written with Olympia's full gaze upon my back, the best thing that I leave the world. Mann stole it, and Kafka stole it, and Hesse stole it, and were talked about. I have been invisible all my life.

I have heard that Kafka mentioned me in the cafés of Prague. I dare say.

You cannot know, *O Leser*, how long it is possible to sit on the side of a bed staring at the floor.

DOKTOR ZWIEBEL looked me dead in the eye. He had the nose of Urbino. Somewhere, deep in his ancestry, back before time began to tick in seconds, when all the earth was a forest of ferns growing in Lake Tchad, there had been a rhinoceros.

— Tell me, Herr Weisel, he began.

— Walser, said I.

— Just so, said Doktor Zwiebel, looking down at the folder before him. Tell me, Herr Walser, you have never I see been married?

— Never, said I, but almost.

I sighed, the doctor sighed.

— How do you mean, *almost?* Remember that anything you tell me goes no further than my files. You are free, indeed I urge you, to tell me all.

— Fräulein Mermet, I said. There was a Fräulein Mermet. I fell in love with her. She regarded me kindly.

— *Pfring! Pfring!* sang the telephone on the desk.

— *Ja? Zwiebel hier.* Seasick? Promethazine hydrochloride and dextroamphetamine sulfate in a little lemon juice. Yes, that is correct. I will look in later. Goodbye. That was the duty officer.

She says a patient who thinks he is Napoleon has run into rough weather off Alexandria. Do you know, Herr Weisel . . .

— Walser.

— . . . that an alarming number of attendants at sanatoria end up as patients? You may know Aufwartender Futter, with a remarkably long head and three moles in a line across his forehead? Just so! He was a patient here for some months, paranoid schizophrenic, thought that everybody in Switzerland was turning into money. He convinced his ward attendant of it, who announced to me one day that he wanted to be put in the bank so as to be drawing interest. Futter thought this was so funny that he emerged from his fantasy, and the two exchanged places, Futter having been fired from his job on the Exchange. Excellent arrangement. Now where were we? You were telling me about your wife, I believe.

— But I didn't marry her.

— Didn't marry who? If she was your wife . . .

— I was about to answer your question, Herr Doktor. You had asked how I was almost married. There was a Fräulein Mermet. I loved her and I believed that she loved me. We wrote many letters to each other. We spent Sunday afternoons in the park. She would fall against my arm laughing for no reason at all. Macaroons . . .

— How many brothers and sisters have you, Herr Weisel?

— Two sisters, Fanny and Lisa, four brothers, Ernst, Hermann, Oskar, and Karl, who is the noted painter and illustrator. He lives in Berlin.

— Your last position seems to have been that of Archivist for the Canton of Bern. Why, may I ask, did you leave?

— I resigned.

— You did not find the pay sufficient or the work congenial?

— We had a difference of opinion as to whether Guinea is in Africa or South America. My superior said I had insulted him. I tied his shoelaces together when he was asleep at his desk one afternoon.

Doktor Zwiebel made a note and fixed it to the folder with a paper clip. Something caught his attention that made him jump. He looked more closely and then glared at me.

— It says here that you have previously been treated for neuroses by one Dr. Gachet, to whom you were recommended by Vin-

cent Van Gogh, and by Dr. Raspail on the advice of V. Hugo.
What does this mean? Did you give this information to the attendant who filled out these forms?

— *Jawohl, Herr Doktor.*

— Then there are Van Goghs still alive? Of the great painter's
family?

— Oh, yes, most certainly. The nephew is very like his uncle,
carrot-haired, *sensitif*, very Dutch.

— And the Hugo here is descended from the noted French
poet?

— That is right.

— And Gachet and Raspail, they are French or Swiss psychia-
trists?

— French.

— How long were you under treatment by them?

POLITICIAN, with rump. Statesman, with nose. Banker, with eye.
You shuffle francs, and stack them, as a priest shifts and settles
Gospel and Graal upon the altar. The clerks at their sacred books,
compounding interest, the vice-presidents, first, second, and third,
all who know the combination of the safe, the tellers with their
sponges, rubber stamps, and bells, these are the only hierophants
left whose rites are unquestioned and unquestionable, whose
sanctions can be laid upon orphan and Kaiser alike, upon factory
and church. Here the shepherd's only ewe and the widow's last
pfennig are demanded, and received, with perfect comfort of con-
science and thrill of rectitude surpassing the adoration of Abraham
honing his knife.

In 1892, when I was fourteen, I left the Gymnasium and applied
for the post of teller in a bank. In this journey my dog surprised
a young kid, and seized upon it, and I, running in to take hold
of it, caught it and saved it alive from the dog. A letter I sent in
reply to a notice in the *Züricher Zeitung* included a phrase from
Vergil, the noted Mantuan, and listed as references Hetty Green
and J. Pierpont Morgan. I was nevertheless instructed by return
post to appear for an interview. I had a great mind to bring it
home if I could; for I had often been musing whether it might be
possible to get a kid or two and so raise a breed of tame goats,

which might supply me when my powder and shot should be all spent.

At the bank I was taken in hand by a kind of assistant priest and put in a gorgeous room to wait for my interview. I had never seen such a carpet, such high windows, or so polished an inkstand.

A door opened. A man in a Roman helmet, leaning on a bamboo cane, limped in. He had cut himself shaving and a sticking plaster, blood at its edges, ran the length of his cheek.

— You are Robert Walser? he asked, reading from a card.

I said I was.

— We are in Albania, he intoned, near the slopes of Ararat. I am the Third Vice-President. Our cellars are full of gold, silver, stocks, notes. As there is a God . . .

And then the door was filled with people, a man with lots of whiskers, clerks, bald men wringing their hands.

— Get him! said Whiskers. Take him to my office. Schmidt, I have told you and told you!

They took the Third Vice-President away, with some effort, leaving me to the gaze of a man who looked at me from top to toe, with disapproval.

— Those shoes, he said, will never do.

RUFZEICHEN in alpine hat, tweed jacket, plus fours, Austrian walking shoes with shredded and tasseled tongues, a stout stick, cigar, monocle, green knit gloves. I came behind in my black English butler's suit, bowler and umbrella, carrying a picnic basket and a plaid rug.

The count held up his hand without looking back.

— Here, he said.

I spread the rug over meadow flowers and laid the count a place. The silverware tinkled strangely in the fine emptiness of the out of doors. The wineglass would not sit straight. Gnats assembled around the count.

I stood at a respectful distance.

— I tell you, Robert, he said through a mouthful of sandwich, these things did not happen before you came. No, I assure you, they did not, decidedly did not. Our cook Claribel is, I believe, possessed.

— Possessed, your lordship?

— Salt in my coffee, eggshells in the omelet, a glove in the soup . . .

— Most distressing.

— It is mad.

It occurred to me then, who could say why, that the dinosaurs I had been reading the count about from a British magazine were not great lizards but chickens as large as a Lutheran church. No one has seen their skins, or, as it may be, their feathers. Only bones survive. They had three toes, long necks, beaks, dainty forelegs which were possibly wings as useless as a dodo's. It may have been the count's savaging of a chicken wing that supplied the idea.

I mentioned the possibility to him, by way of conversation. We were, after all, the only living creatures in miles, give or take a remote eagle and a swarm of gnats.

He gave me a very strang look.

Human nature cannot write. *Ich schrieb das Buch, weil sie mir nicht gestattete, meine Tage in ihrer Nähe zu verbringen, mich ihr zu widmen, was ich mit wahrer Lust getan hätte.* And in the irony of money all ironies are lost.

Potina, Roman deity altarless and distracted, had, in the way of the gods, neither watch, calendar, nor sense of time. She dropped down into the streets of Bern one day, in front of a trolley which almost struck her. Her dress was a thousand years out of fashion, a white wool smock brown with age and riddled hem to yoke by moths who had nibbled the diapered stole of Julia Domna and the stockings of Victoria. Her duty among the immortals was the digestion by infants of their first spoonful of pabulum, whether Ashanti mothers chewing sago and letting it into their babies' mouths, Eskimo matrons poking blubber down pink gullets, or Helvetian mamas spooning into lips open as wide as an eaglet's goat cheese and honey.

Whatever, whenever, wherever she was, Dea Potina rubbed her eyes. These dark places behind doors, these wagons that rolled without oxen: these people had married into the gods. She smelled lightning everywhere and saw lamps burning inside crystal fruit, without air to feed the flame. *Apollon!* she prayed, *spell me those written words.* And the old voice with the cave echo in it, and the snake hiss, told her that the words said, all of them, one way or another, *coin.*

But that building is surely a temple. In truth, said Apollon. They are all temples, and all built to hold coins. Then, she said, I am in the country of the dead, and yet I see smiling children, and I smell lightning, which is never of the underrealm. It is the fashion now, Apollon said, to live as if all were Domos Hades. Some ages fancied the ways of the Olympian gods, some the Syrian Mother, some the wastes of Poseidon, some the living gold of wheat and light and children.

Now they have cut from Dis's realm his gleaming metals and his black slime, his sulphur and salts and poisons, murderous things that they seem to enjoy. But most of all they fancy coin.

EINE ANSICHTSKARTE (Manet's *Monet in His Studio Boat*) from Olympia: Yesterday I saw a woman on the streetcar with her little boy who had his head stuck in his chamber pot and was being taken to the doctor to have it pried off. It was over his eyes and ears, and all you could see of him was his mouth open and howling. His mama was in tears, as was her son, though it was probably *pipi* she kept wiping away. *Herzlich,* Ollie.

IN THE ETERNAL July of Egypt a scribe once wrote on papyrus *she was more comely in her body than all the other women in this world*—a FEATHER, *ah,* and a COIL OF ROPE, *oo,* she, a SHEPHERD'S CROOK and a LOAF, *sett,* was, a LUTE, ASP, and MOUTH, *nefer,* comely, an OWL, *m,* in, a TWISTED ROPE, LOAF, ARM, SHOULDER, THREE, SEATED WOMAN, SHEPHERD'S CROOK and LOAF, *hatset,* her body, MOUTH, *er,* than, BOLT, LOAF, and SEATED WOMAN, *set,* more than, VAGINA, LOAF, and SEATED WOMAN, *khemt,* woman, BOWL and LOAF, *nebt,* any, WATER, LOAF, and DUALITY, *enti,* who, OWL, *m,* in, DUCK, *pa,* the, LAND, *ta,* world, GRAIL, MOUTH, and ASP, *terf,* entire.

He wrote, sighed, and passed the leaf to a binder, who stitched it to the next leaf and rolled it around a stick. An *anu* read the line various evenings to the dash of a seshsesh and the indolent whine of a sa, and lords listened, their brown hands on their square knees, and ladies listened, a *hen* of flowers in their hair, and the shadow of Neb whom the children of darkness call the Sphinx slid from west to east three hundred and sixty-five thousand times and again as many, and again, and who then could read the writing of the scribe?

THUNDER underground began to boom at midnight on the ninth of January 1784 like a hundred batteries of cannon beneath the silver city of Guanaxuato in Mexico, continuing like a ripening summer storm, clap and drum roll, like the hoofbeats of Visigoth cavalry under Alaric coming upon Rome when a havoc of light in midday blue had signaled Vortumna and the Arvals that the hill gods were turning their shoulders from Roman flour and Roman flower, an angry, angled slender crack of fire and a sizzling split through the air and Rome was no longer under the ax and stick pack and eagle and wolf but under the Crow, a sound like high promontories breaking away from a headland and falling into a raging sea. Which awful noise lasted until the middle of February. When, after the third day, no earthquake followed the persistent subterranean thunder, *el cabildo* kept the people inside the city, ringing it with militia, for fear that thieves would come and steal their silver, not an ingot of which shivered in that incongruous stillness and steadfastly detonating tumult.

Yet it was a land where a tall cathedral might suddenly ring all its bells and sink out of sight into a crevice open so briefly that, having swallowed an orchard, a mule train, the church, a sleeping hog, and the local astrologer, it could close again neatly enough to catch a hen by both feet in the pavement of the Calle San Domingo.

Der Graf Rufzeichen sat listening to these details from von Humboldt's *Cosmos* with glassy eyes.

— Avenues of trees, I went on, become displaced in an earthquake without being uprooted. Fragments of cultivated ground of very different kinds mutually displace each other.

— *Erstaunlich!*

— A still more remarkable and complicated phenomenon is the discovery of utensils belonging to one house in the ruins of another at a great distance, a circumstance that has given rise to lawsuits.

— Earthquakes, is it, you're reading me about? asked the Count. My God. I once came all over dizzy while out riding, for no cause except perhaps the game I'd had at old Fuchtel's might have been a touch high, and saw two of everything, and keeled over out of the saddle, stars everywhere. Do you think that was earthquake?

— Did anyone else note a tremor? I asked him.

— How could they? said the Count with some indignation. They weren't there.

— Earthquakes are fairly extensive. They cover quite an area, I believe.

— Couldn't have been a small one there under my horse?

The Count milked his moustache and stared into the corner of the room.

ONCE UPON A TIME, in a Swiss valley, there was born to an honest couple a baby that had a jack-o'-lantern for a head. The parents were sure their grief and horror were the greatest ever felt, and yet the infant suckled and cried, slept and burbled, like any other. Its eyelets were elfin in outline, the neat small triangular nostrils were not really repulsive, and the round hole of a mouth took in its mother's milk with a will and let out boisterous cries that for timbre and volume were the equal of any baby in Switzerland.

For months it was kept hidden. Its parents had come to adore it, as a child sees the greatest winsomeness and charm in a doll that has buttons for eyes, whose mouth is stitched onto cheese-cloth, and whose hair is thread. They ventured to show it to its grandparents, who collapsed in fear and loathing, but who eventually were won over, and loved to dandle little Klaus on their knees.

One by one the neighbors fell down breathless, their eyes rolled back in their heads, at the sight of the little chap and his pumpkin grin, and one by one they got used to him. In no time at all the whole village thought nothing at all of Klaus, and in due course he became a model little boy, quick to learn in school, gratifyingly pious in church, and a fine fellow to all his friends, of whom he had many.

It was then only the rare tinker or traveler who, passing through, caught sight of him and fell screaming into a fit or froze as still as stone and had to be revived with slaps and brandy.

Kafka stole his cockroach from that story. He has, I admit, improved upon it, and seen it from a dark angle. I meant that we are all monsters: by fate and by character. Fate and character are bow and string. What happens to us is what our character invites, guides in, challenges. All that ought to matter is that we are alive, which turns out, I've found, to be our last consideration. What does a banker care whether he is living or dead, so long as he has a shilling to kiss, a franc to lick?

And of life we can ask but continuity. That, as I explain to my doctors, is my neurosis. I have been, I am, I shall be, for awhile, but off and on, like a firefly.

I confuse my doctors. When they say I am mistaken about reality it is they who are mistaken. They say I cannot distinguish, cannot sort fact from fiction.

How solemnly their empty chairs listened to them, and the portraits of Freud and Jung on the wall! The lamps, and especially the fire in the grate, listened to these strange words with dismay. To think that the custodians of the spirit should have prepared for me a categorical prison.

— Consider! I said.

They looked at each other, Doktor Vogel and Doktor Hassen-fuss.

It says in the pages of Mach that the mind is nothing but a continuity of consciousness. It is not itself a thing, it is its contents, like an eye and what it sees, a hand and what it holds. Mach's continuity, like Heraklit's river, defines itself by its flow.

Doktor Vogel looked at Hassenfuss.

— A charming poetic image, he said.

— It is so obvious, I persisted, once you have seen it. The mind is what it knows! It is nothing else at all, at all.

I RESOLVED to hold fast by a piece of the rock and so to hold my breath, if possible, till the wave went back; now as the waves were

not so high as at first, being near land, I held my hold till the wave abated, and then fetched another run, which brought me so near the shore that the next wave, though it went over me, yet did not swallow me up as to carry me away, and the next run I took, I got to the mainland, where, to my great comfort, I clambered up the clifts of the shore and sat me down upon the grass, free from danger, and quite out of the reach of the water.

Commit a word to paper and God knows what you have done. They will read it in Angoulême, in Anchorage, and Hippo. Spiritual crockery for missionary tables in the Cameroons serves quite as well a Mandarin palate. The sheik of Aqbar gathers his twenty sons around him, his five wives and twelve daughters, and reads them the *Encyclopedia Britannica,* a page where it says that phoronids, which comprise the phylum Phoronida, are little-known marine invertebrate animals characterized by an elongated, nonsegmented body that is topped by a tuft of tentacles. Each adult lives within a membranous tube to which sand particles, shells, and other materials may adhere. A king will read a baker's proverbs who could not be invited to supper by the meanest file clerk of the Fish and Vegetables Revenue Branch.

The black hunchback Aesop would never be allowed to stump on his crutch into this library, nor shaggy blind barefoot Homer leaning on a boy, nor staggering Li Po in his dragon silks, nor honest Benjamin Franklin could I introduce into this library without getting fired for exposing *der Graf* to the Gadarene hog. Yet here were their books, bound in red leather.

Weder antik Fisch noch spartanisch Athlet.

— Mad, aren't they? Herr Rufzeichen asked of the ceiling, blowing loops of cigar smoke upward.

— Mad, your lordship?

— These book writers, Robert, that you read me. They are all peculiar, to you and me I mean, wouldn't you say?

STEEP WIND at my throat, my gaze on dizzy shires and canals below, I heard with one ear the tympany of our cold oscillation through crowding gusts and with the other the Eroica. You do not, Meng Tse said, climb trees to look for fish. Nor discover weight with a yardstick or length with a scales. Why were Cassirer and I floating across Europe in a balloon?

— *Hsing!* Cassirer said.

A carp by Hokusai, a spray of maple red as wine, *sao shu* dropping like wistaria down the print. It is *hsing,* Cassirer said by the stove, to desire a wife, plum brandy, gingko jam, and water chestnuts. *Hsing* is internal, justice and mercy external, *nei wei.*

In China as in Greece the epic known in every house and assembly, he explained, is of *Wanderung.* The manner of a people's foraging becomes the *Heldenfahrt* of the *Kollektivunbewusste.* A hero without a journey is like a saint without a vision. Tripitaka and Monkey through a persimmon forest under blue humps of mountains. Herakles mothernaked raising his mouseburrow ox arm in grace to a frisking centaur, wolfwary Ulysses offering his lie to the *meerstrandbewohnend Phaiakischhof,* Cassirer the image peddler and Walser the *Nachnietzschischprosaschriftsteller* aloft in a balloon drifting to the Baltic sands: heroes in our day must take to the ice wastes of the poles, the depths of the sea, the air. We are not certain whether von Moltke's heroism is in his railroad tracks, his invention of general orders, or his translating Gibbon.

He talked of Nietzsche and Semmelweis. The one exhorted us to dream of barefoot Greeks dancing in masks before the enigmas of fermentation and electricity, the other taught us to wash our hands when delivering babies.

Here, in the snow, which would I prefer to walk with me, as if I could heed another ghost, or if Seelig, kind Seelig, were not enough? A man's quality might well be in the sort of misery he has seen with pity. In that case, Semmelweis. Or was it rather Nietzsche? And both were maddened by stupidity. Not I.

I wander out every afternoon, the same way, and have my walk. Every day now for twenty-seven years. Could I once have written books? Once drifted across Europe in a balloon? Once been a butler in Silesia? Was I once a boy?

I watch the linnet, the buck hare, the mountains pink and grey above level mist that lies out from the property wall like a lake of clouds, like the mind's surface before a warmth of thought, light, melts that haze of ghost wool, incertitude of fear.

I ASK AN ATTENDANT who the man is who dances around the grounds and has such anguish in his eyes. He tells me it is the great Nijinsky, schizophrenic paranoid.
— He thinks he is a horse.

WHY SHOULD THIS wild whirl of snow keep us from our walk? It reminds me of the toys in my father's shop, pigeon-breasted Switzers with halberds and cockades, milkmaids in porcelain aprons, shepherds with mouse-faced sheep. O ravelment and shindy of snow on the toy shop's windows! There was an enameled *staffetta* I coveted with real lust: he had a leather hat, a coat as red as cherries, and saddlebags stamped with the arms of the canton.

A rabbit! See him tease a casualness into his fear. Don't move. I can think, as still as he, snow raining upon us both, of a battalion of red soldiers on my father's shelves, of a mandarin poet rolling along the Great Wall in a cart, of Robinson Crusoe conversing with his parrot. But what moves in his mind, the rabbit? Is the image of me on his retina all that he sees, an old man with a face as wrinkled as a pocket handkerchief used for a month? Can he see cabbages and carrots and blackberries? His doe?

It was a day this cold that I saw a lady with a *panache* of pheasant and egret jutting from a swirl of scarlet silk around her hat, and felt my little man suffuse with benevolence, grow long and rise. The colors of coats and scarves in shops, of signs and stone, of tramway and light became splendid. It takes the animal in us to lead the spirit a dance.

Schicksal, Zeit, Unfall: the important thing is to tie one's shoelaces, sew back the parted button, and look the world in the eye.

But the rabbit can think without disregarding all that is characteristic of life, for the infinity of qualifications arising from our thoughts of death is nowhere in his green brain. Yet he is as fearful as if I were a banker, a philanthropist, or a psychiatrist. He lasts, we wear. He leaps, we endure.

The past, I have known for years, is the future. All that has mattered is a few moments, uncongenial while they happened, that turned to gold in the waves of time. February light, that for all its debility might have come from the daytime moon as much as from a red sun beyond a texture of bamboo and chinaberry, fell cold on a wall that bore a French print of a flatfish, a map of the Hebrides, a bust of T. Pomponius Atticus, a Madagascan parrot whose green eye glowed like an opal, and a speckled mirror that reflected on so dull an afternoon nothing except some elemental neutrality of light and dark, vicinity, and patience.

I am most inside outside. Once Olympia said from her repose on the wall that Monsieur Manet was a man women liked. He put them at ease by paying the right kind of attention. He stayed inside himself and looked out. He did not even know how to come outside himself. You could always feel that. It is a comfort to a woman, she said, to see a man so unconsciously himself. A woman knows when to be inside and when to be outside, her mother's only useful lesson, and of course when to be neither.

The snow is a kind of music. Were I ever to write again, perhaps a poem as deft and transparent as one by a Chinese, I would like to witness to the beauty of the snow.

And their books, these people who keep writing, who reads them? It is now a business like any other. I try not to bore them with an old man's talk when they come, the few who want to ask me about writing, about the time before both the wars, about Berlin. I do not tell them how much of all that misery was caused by writers, by men who said they were writers. I do not tell them that I quit writing because I had nothing at all, any more, to say.

There are the tracks of the rabbit. I think they said at the table that today is Christmas. I do not know.

But let us desist, lest quite by accident we be so unlucky as to put these things in order.

Library of Congress Cataloging in Publication Data
Davenport, Guy.
    Da Vinci's bicycle.

    Contents: The Richard Nixon Frieschütz rag.—
C. Musonius Rufus.—The wooden dove of Archytas.
[etc.]
    I. Title.
PZ4.D2457Dad [PS3554.A86]   813′.5′4   78–20513
ISBN 0–8018–2208–4
ISBN 0–8018–2220–3 pbk.